The
Unjust
Justice
System

The Unjust Justice System

Copyright © 2021 Angela Moody Printed in the USA
ISBN (Print Version): 978-1-7364495-1-6

Contents

For Tiffani

The person who helped me find my good.

Chapter 1
Murderer

Every headline across the country read the same. "Woman escapes in a stolen U-Haul truck after killing her husband." I couldn't watch television or listen to the radio without hearing all the horrible things said about me.

"Murderer."

"Burn in hell."

Groups of people chanted outside of the jailhouse as they waited for me to be extradited to Arizona so they could get a look at the woman who killed her husband.

I must be visibly horrifying to be able to do such a thing to my husband, and each person wanted to be the first to get a glimpse or snap a photo of the horrible woman sitting in their local county jail. My confession to Bryan's murder was a big deal in our small rural Indiana community. Nothing like this happened around here. People were treating the story like a serial killer had just confessed to multiple unsolved murders. My mugshot was on every television station and every newspaper across the country. Everyone could hear a play-by-play of my extradition on the radio stations from Indiana to Arizona. But not one person, not one reporter or radio personality, spoke about the real reason behind why I confessed to Bryan's murder.

Not a single one of them talked about the abuse or that I possibly confessed unwillingly.

I was alone in this. Strangers wanted me to be hung from a tree. Reporters used words to describe me that I had never even heard. I was a monster in the eyes of the public, and not once did anyone ask what happened or why it happened.

Mr. Andrews made me believe that he was on my side and that he would represent my confession in a way that would hopefully give me a better chance at a future someday. Little did I know, but Mr. Andrews didn't care about my story. All he cared about was getting a confession from me. Mr. Andrews had only been a public defender for a couple of years when he received my case. He needed to make a name for himself if he was ever going to rise in the ranks as a prosecutor or even a judge. My case was his one case of fame that he would carry throughout his career. His one break that he would keep in his back pocket for years to come as he moved himself up the latter. I was his steppingstone, and it didn't matter to him if I was innocent or confessed to protect my children. I was the one case and confession he needed.

Mr. Andrews formally typed my recorded confession and asked me to sign it. I assumed it was a formality, so I signed without hesitation.

"You are still going to play my recorded confession, right?"

"Of course. Your signature makes everything official."

My recorded confession was never presented to Mr. Andrews's supervisors, only the written confession. I trusted that he wrote out my confession word for word, and I didn't need to read it. I knew what it said.

Unfortunately, the written confession was a watered-down version of my recorded one. Everyone's hatred for me made sense now. The community knew nothing about the abuse or about the prosecutor's office trying to bring charges on my children. All they knew was an evil woman sat awaiting extradition in their local county jail. I was a murderer, a monster to them, and I deserved whatever sentence I got.

Angel still couldn't visit me in jail because of her age, and her visits to the sidewalk outside of my cell stopped because we were concerned about her safety. I missed her; I missed talking to her every day. Jail is a lonely place. You wouldn't think that because you are around so many people and there is constant movement, it isn't the same as having people you love and trust. In county jail, people are continually coming and going, so you don't have an opportunity to get to know them. I knew I would be leaving soon, and the last thing I wanted was to have to say good-bye to another person I cared for.

So, I stuck to myself and read many books, hoping to get my high school diploma one day. Maybe something good would come out of my incarceration.

"You have a call from a county corrections facility. Do you accept this call?"

"I accept the call." Angel answered.

"Hi, Sis. How are you?"

"I am okay. I got in a fight at school today."

"Don't be fighting. You can't afford to get kicked out of school.

"I know, Mom, but this girl is a bully, and I have had enough of her crap. No one understands that my mom is in jail, and I am going to be an orphan and homeless soon."

"I am still trying to sort things out. I will always be your mother, no matter what. You are not an orphan."

"I know, but you can't do anything from jail, and you definitely can't when they take you to Arizona. I am all alone, Mom."

"I am sorry that you have to go through this too. I didn't have a choice, Angel. The alternative was to have you and Adam on trial with me. I didn't know what else to do."

"I know you didn't have a choice. I am not mad at you. I don't know what to do at this point. I can stay with the Toney's, but then I will have to change schools, again. I don't have anyone here that will take me in for the next year and a half. I am not ready to grow up, but it looks like I have no choice."

"We will figure this out. I promise. Please stay in the apartment until the landlord kicks you out. Pay the rent with the Social Security money. I have to go. I will call tomorrow. I love you, Sis."

"I love you too, Mom."

I sat in the county jail for six months before my extradition to Arizona. The constant chatter outside the jailhouse had finally fizzled out. I was soon forgotten.

The morning my extradition was to take place, I was awoken at 5 am by a deputy and served breakfast in a single holding cell. All my personal belongings were given back to me in a small envelope along with my clothes from the day of my arrest.

"Put your street clothes on. A Marshall will be here soon to transport you to the airport. Once you are dressed, I will come back to get you for a final phone call."

The deputy handed me the bag with my clothes in it. Unwashed, my clothes still smelt like home. I put my shirt up to my face and closed my eyes. I inhaled the smell for a few minutes before I got

5

dressed. I imagined this was all a dream. I was holding onto the last bit of freedom I would have, even if it was just the smell.

The deputy escorted me down the hall to the phone, where I would make my last call from Indiana. I attempted to call Angel, but she was in school, so the call went unanswered. I wanted so desperately to say good-bye. Angel would soon turn 18, but she would not be able to visit me in prison in Arizona. A trip that far would cost a lot of money, and we didn't have it. I was unsure of my future, and I did not know when the next time I would get to see my children's faces. I broke down and cried as I dialed the number to call my mother.

"You have a call from a county corrections facility. Do you accept this call?"

"I accept the call." My mother answered.

"Hi, Mom. I don't have a lot of time. They are getting ready to transport me to Arizona. I tried to call Angel, but she is probably in school."

"I am glad you called. Do you know when your sentencing will be?"

"I have no idea. I am being taken to Maricopa County first, and then I will be transferred to prison once they have sentenced me. I could be in their county jail for months. The process is usually slow."

"I love you, Rachel. I know why you did this, but I

wish you wouldn't have. I worry so much about you. I can't believe one of my children is going to be in prison."

"What is done is done now. I will have to do my best to survive. Watch over Angel, please. I worry about her. She has been fighting at school, and I am afraid she will get herself into some trouble. I have to go, Mom. I love you. I will try to call when I can."

"I love you, too, Rachel." The phone went dead as I held the receiver in my hand.

This was it. I would soon know my fate. The deputy handcuffed me and escorted me to the jailhouse's side door that led into a garage where they stored the transportation vans. A deputy drove the van, while a United States Marshall sat shotgun. He would be my escort on my flight to Arizona. As we pulled out of the garage and turned the corner to head towards the highway, I made a glance at the sidewalk where I last saw Angel.

"Stop! Stop! That is my daughter. Please let me tell her good-bye. Please, I am begging you." Unknowingly, Angel ditched school so that she could see me one last time.

"Ma'am, that is totally against the rules. You are a murderer. I can't just pull over and let you out." The deputy looked over to the Marshall, unsure if he should comply with my request.

"Sir, please. Just slow down so I can see her face one last time." The Marshall nodded, giving the deputy the go-ahead.

The deputy slowed the van to a complete stop up to the sidewalk where Angel stood. Through the glass, we said our good-byes. I put my handcuffed hands up to the window as she met them with hers from the other side.

"I love you, Sis. Everything is going to be okay." I said as tears streamed down my face.
"I love you too." Angel stepped away from the curb.

The deputy slowly started driving away. I kept glancing back as I watched my baby break down on that sidewalk. Thankfully, our friends, the Toney's, embraced her as she fell to her knees. I had to look away. I couldn't witness the heartbreak I had inflicted on my child. It was a gut-wrenching good-bye.

Chapter 2
Extradition

I stayed quiet during the hour and fifteen-minute ride to the airport as I listened to the deputy and Marshall chat about their careers and families. I was scared, unsure, and broken.

As we pulled into the airport parking lot, it appeared as if we had privileged access to the flight. We were met by a security guard who drove us to the runway on a four-seater cart. The Marshall lightly held my arm as we walked up the stairs to the 747 airplane. The rest of the passengers would enter through the airport and security, but my entry was less secure and more discrete. The Marshall grabbed an airplane blanket and draped it over my hands, disguising the handcuffs. He was dressed in all black, but nothing he wore revealed that he was a United States Marshall. Occasionally, I glanced at the gun on his side, probably the reason we had secret access to the plane and didn't go through security, causing attention. I was thankful for the discretion as we were seated in the very last row. I took my seat next to the window, ensuring I could not attempt an escape. The thought never crossed my mind, but I guess this is how they transport all prisoners; I was no different. I was a murderer, after all.

I was awoken by the tires touching the Phoenix airport's pavement after our non-stop flight that only took a couple of hours. As the passengers began exiting the plane, I looked to the Marshall for guidance on our exit.

"We will exit last. It will be a while." The Marshall patted my leg, gave me a slight nod and a crooked grin.

Occasionally a passenger would stare at us as if to wonder why we weren't exiting the plane. Maybe they knew I was a prisoner. I don't really know. We exited similarly to entering the plane. We were escorted to a transportation van in one of the parking garages. Again, I sat in the back as the deputy drove, and the Marshall sat shotgun. This time our drive would be less than 30-minutes.

The heat hit my face as I stepped out of the van and onto the Maricopa County jail grounds. The place was five times the size of the county jail back home. My heart began to flutter as the Marshall led me through the gates, but I knew if I was going to survive, I needed to push my emotions down and appear strong.

The deputies put me through the usual processing, fingerprints, mugshot, and jail-issued clothes. Before taking me to my temporary cell, a woman in a blue, crisp suit met with me in one of the interrogation rooms.

"Mrs. Havens, my name is Ms. Sanchez. I will be representing you during your sentencing hearing here in Arizona. Do you have any questions?"

"When will my sentencing be?"

"We have you scheduled for one week from today. We do not plan to put you in the general population since you will be transported immediately after sentencing. Initiation is usually done in the first week, and there is no need to put you through that when we know you will be gone soon."

"Initiation?"

"You know you are in jail, don't you? The first week is when most prisoners get tested by the other inmates. To see who and where you fit in. Initiation."

"Okay. I guess I know what to look forward to."

"You will be in a single holding cell until then." The attorney sifted through papers she had stuffed in a manila folder, barely making eye contact with me.

"Is the judge going to hear my confession? I had my attorney back home record my confession. I wanted the judge to hear it so he would know what I went through."

"That is really up to the judge. They run thousands of people through this jail every week. I guess you can hope that he is in a good mood and will listen to it; otherwise, he is just going to sentence you. You confessed, and that is all he cares about."

Like Mr. Andrews, Ms. Sanchez was doing a job, and I do not believe she saw me as a person, just a case she needed closed. I am not sure she looked at my case for more than a few minutes before meeting with me. What a lonely and frightening position to be in when the people supposedly fighting for you aren't putting up much of a fight.

I waited out the week in a lonely single cell about the size of a walk-in closet. Occasionally a friendly guard would spend a minute or two chatting with me, but the time drug on. I was anxious to know how many years I would be sitting in prison somewhere in Arizona. I was also fearful, anticipating what prison life was going to be like. Deep down I was terrified.

My sentencing hearing took place on a hot summer Tuesday morning. Tuesdays were reserved for these types of hearings because Mondays were filled with weekend cases. Ms. Sanchez met with me on Monday to review the process. I was ignorant of all the formalities. I had never been to prison, and I did not know what to expect or what to do.

"Rachel, I have made arrangements for you to try on a couple of loaner suits for your hearing. You need to do your best to make a good impression on the judge. Let's hope he is in a good mood tomorrow because your fate lies in his hands."

"I can do that. I think if the judge hears my confession, he will do what is right. Don't you?"

"We can only hope. Try on the suits. I will be back shortly."

The loaner suits were extremely outdated, wrinkled, and smelt musty. How am I supposed to make a good impression in one of these? I thought. It didn't matter at that point. Those suits were what I had to work with, so I made the best of them. I found one that fit well enough that it would do for my hearing. I asked one of the friendly guards if she would hang the suit up so that maybe the wrinkles would somewhat fall out overnight.

I will never forget her. Her name was Fredonia, a sweet older lady who migrated from Mexico when she was a teenager. She told me she had been a guard for over 30 years at that same county jail. She also told me that she had seen thousands of women come through that jail, and I wasn't the typical inmate that she had encountered over the years. She gave me hope that the judge would see that same person she saw. I could only pray that he would.

Fredonia awoke me at 6 am on Tuesday.

"Rachel, wake up. Your hearing is today, and you need to be fresh. Here is your suit."

"The wrinkles fell out," I said excitedly.

"I took it home and ironed it for you. Now get dressed before you get me in trouble." Fredonia whispered.

"Fredonia, I can't thank you enough. You are a wonderful human being. Thank you!"

Fredonia made me feel as if there was still good in this world. She would probably never know what her act of kindness meant to me, and I would never get the chance to show my gratitude for it. At a time in my life when I felt so hopeless, one single person made me feel worthy.

I did my best to fix my hair and look presentable. I still didn't know what to expect. It was time, time to find out my fate. The world had already condemned me, but the true judgment would be in the hands of the presiding judge passing down my sentence that day.

Chapter 3
Sentencing Day

Ms. Sanchez briefly walked by my holding cell before the guards prepared to transport me to the courthouse. She handed me a manila folder with one piece of paper in it. I slowly opened the folder and then looked back up at her, puzzled.

"That is your confession. The judge will ask you if this is your confession. You will only have a few seconds to respond to him. There are many cases today. I will meet you there."
"Wait. What about my recorded confession?" I stood up and looked down the hall in her direction.

Ms. Sanchez had already made it halfway down the hall before I realized that the confession that would be presented to the judge and the one I held in my hand was the watered-down version typed by Mr. Andrews months before. This was not how I saw things going. The judge would never hear my recorded confession. I was devastated.

"Rachel, I am sorry, but I have to put you in shackles. I know you are not dangerous, but it is the rules." Fredonia gently handcuffed my hands and then attached the chains to the shackles around my feet.

"It is time. A van is waiting for us." Fredonia said softly.

"They screwed me. This is not justice." I said as we walked to the van waiting for us outside of the jailhouse.

"What is wrong, Rachel?"

"The judge will never hear my recorded confession. This whole time my attorneys made me believe that I would get fair sentencing because of the abuse. The judge will never know anything about it."

"Are you sure?"

"This fucking piece of paper with one paragraph is all he will hear." I held up the manila folder as tears rolled down my face.

"I will be praying for you, Rachel," Fredonia said as she helped me into the side door of the transportation van.

I shook off my devastation as we drove to the courthouse. Our destination was only a few miles, but the Phoenix traffic and continuous stopping and starting again made it feel like we were taking a much longer journey.

"We are here, Rachel. I will escort you into the courtroom. Don't let it intimidate you. There are many cases on the docket today; we could be here for a long time. I will be with you every minute." Fredonia said, trying to walk me through the process. It seemed she was my only friend.

I could hear the chatter inside from the lobby as several deputies escorted prisoners into the courtroom. The doors must have been twelve feet tall, solid oak with iron handles. It was a beautiful room, although dreadful. Each prisoner, including myself, was seated one by one in the wooden pews that sat behind the two desks strategically positioned towards the presiding judge. Our shackles chimed and clunked against the wood as we took our places. It was apparent that some of these prisoners had been here before. Their faces held less fear than I am sure mine did. I kept looking back, searching for Fredonia. Each time our eyes would meet, she would nod her head and give me a small smile.

To the left of the room were two glass enclosures with a chair and microphone in each. I would soon find out that those enclosures were for the most violent of prisoners. The ones that were so dangerous that having them sitting with the general public was too risky.

One by one, prisoners' names were called by the bailiff. The judge would briefly read their charges and issue their sentences. None were allowed to speak to the judge. I feared mine would be the same.

Hours went by as I watched one prisoner after another meet their fate. I surely didn't have much longer as the courtroom slowly began to clear out.

"Rachel Havens." The bailiff called my name. Ms. Sanchez motioned for me to stand up and make my way to the left side table. She grabbed my arm as I tightly held onto my manila folder.

"Mrs. Havens, you have confessed to the murder of Bryan Havens. Is that correct?" The judge never looked up from his paperwork.

"Yes, sir, but......"

"How can there be any butts? I have your signed confession in front of me." The judge swiftly interrupted.

"I...I..." I froze. The judge's stern conviction of me made me speechless.

"Mrs. Havens, due to the nature of the crime, you are being charged with 2nd-degree murder in the state of Arizona."

"Uh, sir."

"Is there something I left out, Mrs. Havens?" The judge sternly looked up over his reading glasses at me.

"Sir, I was given a plea agreement and a reduced charge of manslaughter. You said 2nd-degree murder."

"I do not have any record of a plea agreement. If you have a copy, I will gladly take a look."

"No, sir, I don't have a copy." Panic came over my face as I looked at Ms. Sanchez. She shook her head; she didn't have a copy either. I stood there in disbelief. The justice system failed me and probably many others as they herded us in like cattle being sent into a slaughterhouse. The disgrace of it was overwhelming.

"Mrs. Havens, if you have nothing further, I would like to continue. I have many more cases before my day is over."

"Please continue." Ms. Sanchez said as I remained silent.

"Again, Mrs. Havens, you are being charged with 2nd-degree murder in the state of Arizona for the murder of your husband, Bryan Havens. Due to the nature of the crime, I am sentencing you to 20 years, with the possibility of parole. You will be given one year of time served. You will serve out the remainder of your sentence in the Perryville state prison. Good day, Mrs. Havens." The judge swung his gavel and motioned for Fredonia to remove me from the courtroom.

I truly believe he knew what sentence he was handing out that day. I don't know if anything I said would have changed the outcome. I was defeated. I would be almost 60 years old before I would be free again. I would miss everything, and a chance at a normal life was not realistic. I was hopeless. I spent my youth tormented by my father and later abused by my husband to spend most of my life in prison. What on earth did I do so wrong to have to endure all that I have?

Fredonia guided me through the courtroom towards the exit door. A side door where a black 15 passenger van with dark tinted windows waited for us. Before I made my way through the door, I glanced back at the courtroom, where only a few people remained. I was taken back when I locked eyes with one of my and Bryan's friends from the mountain. I didn't understand why he was there. Maybe he wanted to ensure that I received the most severe sentence. Was he there to support me or condemn me? I did not know. I am sure the mountain was a buzz when I was arrested for Bryan's murder and later confessed, but it didn't make any sense to me why Jacob, our mutual friend and the only person I knew sitting in that courtroom, would be there for my sentencing. My thoughts raced with uncertainty and confusion, but my focus now had to be on surviving 20 years in prison.

"Best of luck to you, Rachel," Fredonia said as she guided me by the arm onto the van.
"Thank you for everything. You are a wonderful person. I will never forget you, Fredonia."

There were seven other women in that van waiting to be transported to Perryville penitentiary. I was the last to be handed my sentence that day, so I took my seat in the first row opposite the deputy driving the van. Another deputy was positioned in the van's very back, ensuring our arrival to Perryville would happen without incident. It appeared as if some of the other women had taken that trip before. They spoke to one another and about other inmates that they looked forward to seeing upon our arrival. I briefly glanced around the van. I was frightened by these other women except for a young blonde girl, probably not much older than Angel, who sat quietly as she stared out the window. She, too, seemed unsure of what we would encounter upon arriving at the prison. I gently smiled at her as she smiled back.

Perryville prison, located in Goodyear, Arizona, roughly 25 miles from Phoenix, was surrounded by desert. The prison was relatively new, and I heard rumors that the prison was designed to help women develop multiple skills during their incarceration. The warden highly believed in rehabilitation and, therefore, encouraged and implemented numerous programs, including education and skill development programs. I hoped I would be able to busy myself for however long I would be locked up. A straight shot across I-10 from Phoenix, our ride would take over an hour due to the traffic along the way.

I stared out the front window as my mind raced and replayed every detail of my life. In 20 years, all of this would be so different. The cars would be different, the buildings would change, or more buildings would be erected in the many vacant lots that we passed. I wouldn't drive a vehicle for 20 years. My children could be grandparents by the time I am released. It was insane to think that I would have to figure out how to make a life amongst all women from all walks of life. I would miss everything, Angel's graduation, wedding, and the birth of her children. I would miss Adam's successes and adventures. I would be a different person in 20 years and probably forgotten by many of the people I had known and loved throughout my life. The Rachel entering that prison would not be the same one leaving it.

Chapter 4
Cellmate

The gate opened slowly as the van drove onto the prison grounds. A quietness settled in the van as we all gazed out the windows. I imagined my life as a prisoner; others were anticipating a reunion with old friends. Whatever the reason for our silence, it was eerie.

"Everyone out!" The deputy who sat in the back shouted. "Line up single file. If you have anything that you have been able to sneak in this far, I suggest you give it up now. Once we make it through those doors, you belong to Perryville penitentiary."

Several guards met us at the sidewalk that led to the prison doors. Their faces were stern and cold. Multiple rows of barbwire on top of the chain-link fences and the armed guards above was a grim picture of my future. We were shortly greeted by a white male, maybe in his 30's but balding. He couldn't have been much older than me. He was short but stocky as if he worked out daily. His appearance was less than intimidating compared to the stern-faced guards.

"Ladies, my name is Warden Johnson. Welcome to your home for however long you will be here. I have designed this prison to help women accomplish whatever they thought they could have accomplished on the outside. It is up to you to take advantage of the programs I have implemented. If you choose not to participate, you have failed yourself. If you choose to continue the criminal activity that got you here in the first place, you will find yourself spending much of your time alone in solitary confinement. It is up to you how you choose to spend your days here."

I found the wardens welcoming speech encouraging. He seemed like a caring man who believed in rehabilitation. Maybe I could better myself in this dreaded place. Those thoughts still didn't bring me much comfort as we were led through several gates and then a solid metal door. Once the eight of us made it through the door, we were stopped in a long narrow hallway. It was sterile with white concrete cinder blocked walls and white polished tile floors. Two guards waited for us with gloved hands and clear full-face masks.

"Ladies, strip down and place your clothes to the right of you. Turn and face the wall placing your hands on the wall, and spread your legs as far as you can get them. When it is your turn, you will squat as if you are sitting in a chair. Once you have been fully inspected, you will stand up and wait until all of you are finished."

One by one, we were all gone over thoroughly. I have never in my life been touched by another woman in the way the guard touched me. She searched and spread every crack and crevice on my body. It was humiliating.

"You all can turn around now. Keep your hands to your side until you are given your clothes. Your shirt is always to remain tucked in. An untucked shirt constitutes an automatic search. After you are dressed, you will be led to one of the interview rooms, where you will go over your medical records, arrests, etc., with an officer. Once that is complete, we will take you to your home." The guard chuckled with sarcasm.

My interview was brief. I had no medical issues, no previous arrests to speak of, or tattoos. It was apparent that I was a newcomer to prison. Once we completed our interviews, mugshots, and fingerprinting, we were lined up against a wall where we were given our bedroll. The guard gave us one sheet, one blanket, and a flat pillow, one by one. We marched through the prison, similar to what you see in the movies. All eyes were on us as the other inmates looked us over, whistling and cackling. We were each escorted to our cells; my new home would be cell C24. The room was small, with two beds stacked on top of one another, two metal lockers, a stainless-steel sink, and a toilet combo.

Pictures of a family and children were taped to the wall around the top bunk. My cellmate was absent when I arrived, but it appeared she occupied the top bunk. Hesitantly I pushed several items to the side as I sat down on the bottom bed. I was scared to disrupt my cellmate's things, not knowing what reaction she might have. I was new to prison, but I wasn't ignorant that possessions in a place like that were gold and highly guarded.

"Well, looky there. You must be my new celly. I am Jo. J.O., not J.O.E. that is a dude's name." Jo was a big girl. She must have been 5'10 and weighed well over 250lbs. Her entire body was covered in tattoos, and her hair was a man's buzz cut.
"I am Rachel."
"Whatcha in for, Rachel. Here let me move this stuff. I have been alone for a bit, so I just put my things wherever."
"Murder," I responded.
"No, shit. Who did you kill?"
"I didn't kill anyone. I am innocent."
"Right. We are all innocent in here." Jo giggled.
"Can I take a nap? I am so tired after today."
"Shit, girl, you can take a nap whenever. You don't have anything to do."
"I think I will do that." I smiled gently at Jo.

Despite Jo's appearance, she was a jolly person. She seemed accommodating and welcoming. I was

26

thankful that I didn't have to fend off anyone my first day. I needed to rest, and I needed kindness after all I had been through. Jo let me rest as she quietly read in the bunk above me. Occasionally she would laugh out loud and then noticeably reserve her laughter. I did my best to rest my eyes and body, but the surrounding noise kept my sleep light. My mind raced as I went in and out for about two hours.

"You are awake? Cool, I am anxious to get to know you." Jo said after I sat up on the edge of my bed.
"There isn't much to know. I am not that exciting."
"We will have plenty of time for that anyway. So, is this your first time?"
"Yes. I have been in a county jail for about six months, and I did a day or two here and there, but I have never been to prison."
"Cool. Well, I can teach you everything you need to know, but first, let's cover our roommate situation." Jo's eyes widened as she jumped down from the top bunk.
"Okay."
"I sleep on the top bunk. I don't like people touching my shit, so if something of mine is in your way, then you need to ask me to move it. I don't like messy. We will clean once a week, but don't leave your shit lying around the rest of the time. You need something, I can get it, but don't take it from me. That is a threat. I don't like thieves. I know most of

the people in this place that can get us whatever we want so, ask me first. Don't bring your drama up in here. Nobody messes with me in here, so if you're going to stay away from that crap, stay close to me." Jo babbled on as she tidied up our small cell.

"Okay."

"You are scared, aren't you?"

"Shitless."

"It's not that bad once you get used to it. I have been here five or six years now. Shit, I quit counting." Jo laughed.

"Why are you here?" I asked.

"That is a long screwed-up story."

"I don't have shit to do. I am listening." We both laughed.

"I think I will like you. You got a sense of humor. Maybe I will tell you after chow. I am fucking starving. I wish they would hurry up already." Jo looked down the hall.

"Will we go somewhere, or do they bring it to us?"

"Damn, you are new. We will go to the chow hall. You can eat in here, but you need to get out and see some folks, or you are going to go crazy."

"Alright."

"Don't worry. Ain't nobody going to mess with you when you are with me."

"What makes you so sure of that?"

"I am their dude." Jo giggled.

"What?"

"I know you think that I am gay and all based on

my appearance, but that is the farthest from the truth. I like dudes. I keep my look this way to keep them off my back. They respect me and think of me as a dude. So, I let them."

"Okay. I guess I understand."

"Alright, let me explain it this way. I take care of a lot of people here. They need something; I get it for them. They give me something back, and I give it to someone who wants that thing. I play the system. The lesbians all want to be with me, but I make them think I got a girl. For the most part, they leave me alone. I am the middleman, so they ain't going to just cut me out. I am their supplier for everything from menstrual pads to cigarettes. They will soon think you are my girlfriend, and I would advise you to make them believe it. What we do alone is none of their business, but if they think you are taken, especially by me, they will leave you alone."

"But I am not a lesbian."

"You will soon learn that in here, everyone is a lesbian." Jo laughed. "Let's go eat."

I hesitantly followed behind Jo as she led us to the chow hall, as she called it. Lots of people stared and greeted Jo as we passed by. It did seem she had a lot of admirers, and she strutted as if she knew it. Jo's personality was unlike anyone I had ever met. She was firm in the way she spoke but kind too. People seemed to be drawn to her. Her personality was powerful and admirable. Walking through that prison, I was thankful that the person I would be sharing my time within the prison was her.

"Hey Sally, how is it going? I haven't seen you in a while, and dang, you are looking good. Give my girl a little extra today. She just got here, and it has been a rough one." The girl behind the food counter glanced over at me and then slopped an extra scoop on my tray.
"Thank you." I said softly.
"See, I told you. Stick with me."

We quietly ate as several other women dropped cupcakes and pies off to Jo, as she discretely stuck them in her waistband and then winked at me. I quickly understood that Jo was the dealer in that prison. She was dealing everything from cupcakes to toothbrushes. She was highly respected, and I needed to learn as much as I could from her. We finished eating and then chatted with a few of Jo's friends before retreating to our cell.

"Are you in here for a long time? You seem to be comfortable with your situation." I asked Jo.
"I don't have a choice. I am serving life."
"Oh, wow." I shockingly said.
"You have to make a decision about how you are going to do your time. You can sit around and sulk and feel sorry for yourself if you want, but the truth is your life can be decent in here."

"I hope someday I can feel that way too."

"Hey, we all go through it in the beginning. This shit sucks. I ain't going to lie, I went through it too, but I had to figure out how to make the best of it. Some people never do."

"So, what changed it for you?"

"Pastor Mel."

"Who is Pastor Mel?"

"I will introduce you on Sunday. She is our prison Pastor. She is one of us, but she changed my life."

"Is she going to try to save me? I already got saved back home in a small church and baptized in the creek."

"She doesn't push any of her beliefs. She tells it how it is and lets you decide."

"Okay. I am going to need something. I feel hopeless."

"Each day will get better. Hang in there."

"So, what got you life?"

"Love and a man. A stupid fucking man."

"Did you kill him?"

"I wish. I would probably have been out by now."

"Do you care to tell me what happened? I don't think I will be able to sleep tonight."

"What do you want to know?"

"Tell me everything. Start from the beginning."

"Alright. Damn, like a bedtime story." Jo giggled.

"Yeah, start from childhood."

"I came from a great family. My parents were hard-working middle-class folks. My sister and I were in every sport you can imagine, and my mom and dad came to every game no matter what. During my junior year in high school, my parents were killed in a car accident. My sister was away in college at the time, trying to figure her life out. After they passed, my sister and I tried to hold everything together, but we were both still young. They had life insurance, which paid our house off and left us a little money. My sister didn't want to come back to take care of me because she had a boyfriend and all, so I convinced her that I could take care of myself and finish school. I did pretty good for a while. I went to school, stayed in sports, and fed myself. I had a part-time job that helped with the extras. All was good until I met Martin.

Martin was Latino, with dark hair, smooth skin, and sexy as sexy gets. I fell hard for him, and he did me too. He was five years older than me, but no one was around to tell me I couldn't date him with no parents and all. We were a true love match. I can't even describe how we were together. Damn, that shit makes me get into my feelings. Anyway, after about a year of dating him, I found out that he was in an L.A. gang. I mocked it at first because he was so sweet and kind that I couldn't imagine him in a gang of any kind, and I surely couldn't imagine him hurting anyone. I later found out that he was a high-ranking member. Like he was deep in that shit. He was the one making decisions to kill people. I couldn't believe it. I broke up with him. I was so hurt, but my parents didn't raise me that way. They were good Christian folks.

Martin and I stayed away from each other for about three months, but I couldn't shake him. I was so in love with him that I took him back. We went right back to being the way we were together. All was good, and he kept me away from the violence and crimes for a while.

After I graduated high school and turned 18, he started taking me on deals with him. I helped him rob some people, steal cars, bikes, and small crimes like that. It was kind of exciting. My parents sheltered me, so I didn't know anything about that type of lifestyle. It was all new to me, and Martin protected me for the most part.

I remember that day like it was yesterday. Martin and I was just riding around with another gang member. We stopped at a gas station to get some drinks. The next thing I know, Martin is robbing the store. The clerk pulled out a bat for protection, and Martin shot him. They ran out, but I stood there in shock. Martin came back and yelled at me to get in the car. I couldn't believe it. I had never seen anything like that.

So, it ended up that the only footage the cops had was of me going in and leaving the store. Martin let me take the fall for it because I wouldn't snitch on him or his friend. I think they sent me here because of my affiliation with the gang. If they put me in an

L.A. prison, I would have no choice but to join the gang in prison and continue committing crimes."

"That is deep. You are innocent. I am sorry that happened to you."

"I am not completely innocent. I did steal from people, and there is nothing that I hate more than a thief. So, I am guilty of those things, but I never killed anyone."

"Me either. Someday I will tell you how I ended up here. Good-night, Jo."

Chapter 5
Pastor Mel

Sunday morning Jo and I ate breakfast and then quickly met up with about twenty other women in a small meeting room. Jo introduced me to several of them as we took our seats. There was a hodgepodge of women in that room, all different races, and all different backgrounds. Every one of us was searching for something while serving our time. We were searching for peace and comfort amid the steel prison bars.

"Good morning, ladies." Pastor Mel said with a warm smile.

Pastor Mel was a large black woman. She was every bit 6'3 and probably played basketball before she became a pastor in prison. I wanted to get to know her and learn about how she ended up in a place like this and then became a pastor. It seemed the more I talked to other women, the more I learned about how the justice system failed them; it failed all of us.

"Today, we are going to skip the singing, ladies. I want to get right into the word. My heart has been heavy this week, and God has put some things on my mind that need to be said." Pastor Mel opened her bible and looked down briefly at her notes.

"The Lord said, "Come to me, all who are weary and heavy-laden, and I will give you rest." Aren't we all weary in this place? Aren't we all feeling the heaviness that sits on our chests and torments our minds? He says, come to me. Are you turning to him? Are you seeking him, or are you trying to understand your circumstances on your own? The bible tells us that all things work out for good for those that love the Lord. Now you might say, "Pastor Mel, there is no good coming from being locked up." I say the devil is a liar. All things, the bible says. Not just when you are home with your families, not only when you are working and building a life. All things.

We must all learn to have faith in the things to come and the things unknown and unseen. You are here today for a reason. I know some of you have been wrongly convicted, and I know that bitterness has devoured you. I know some of you have committed unspeakable crimes, and you can't forgive yourselves. I know some of you have hatred so deep in your soul that you don't see how you could ever forgive the wrongs that have been done to you. I know these things because I, too, have felt them all. But I am here to tell you that there is a better way. A way to forgive yourself and forgive others. A way to start doing the good that God has intended for you, even in this place. Today is a new day, ladies—a day of peace and a day of forgiveness.

Lay your burdens at the feet of our Lord Almighty, and let him fight your battles. Give it all to him and release the heaviness that weighs you down. Today is a day to rejoice because you are free through Christ Jesus, our Lord, and Savior even though you are locked up. Can I get an amen?"

"Amen!" We all shouted.

I felt every bit of Pastor Mel's sermon. All the things she said were exactly how I was feeling that very moment. It was like she was in my head and knew what to say to me. My emotions let loose, and I couldn't control myself as I began sobbing. I was touched by God, by Pastor Mel, I don't know, but I sat in that hard metal chair and poured my heart out.

"Please, Lord, get me through this. I can't do it on my own. I need you, Lord. I am scared, I am heartbroken, and I am lost."

When I looked up from my prayer, several women huddled around me, including Jo and Pastor Mel. All of them were jointly praying for me and standing on my behalf in prayer to God. It was unreal. They didn't know me, they didn't know what I had done, but they all believed that I was worthy of God's love and their love. It was overwhelming and precisely what I needed.

Jo and I walked back to our cell, never speaking a

word. I am sure she knew how broken I felt. Her story was like many others, yet she decided to embrace her incarceration and do all the good she could do in such a terrible place. I admired her, and I was thankful for her.

"I need to talk to my daughter. Where can I go to make a phone call?" I asked Jo.

"I will show you. Come on."

"You have a call from Perryville penitentiary. Do you accept this call?"

"Yes, yes, I accept the call." Angel shouted into the phone.

"Your call is being recorded."

"Mom."

"Hi, Sis. I miss you."

"Where are you?"

"I am at Perryville, in Goodyear, Arizona."

"Are you okay? How much time did you get?"

"I am fine. My cellmate is nice and helpful. The judge gave me twenty years."

"They gave you twenty years. How can they do that?"

"The judge never heard my recorded confession, just the one Mr. Andrews typed out. It didn't say anything about the abuse, only that I confessed to Bryan's murder."

"That is so unfair, Mom. I can't believe they can do such a thing."

"It is just the way the system works. They need to get cases closed as fast as they can. I was just a case to them. I will be fine, though. Do not worry about me. I am more worried about you."

"I am okay, Mom. I graduate in a few months. I wasn't going to walk at graduation, but Mr. Howell insisted that I do."

"I am proud of you. Mr. Howell is a good man, and I am glad he wants you to do that."

"I don't know what the point is. No one will be there for me. Mr. Howell pulled me into his office this week, and I thought I was in trouble, but he told me that he heard I wasn't going to go to graduation because I didn't have a cap and gown. He gave me a cap and gown and said he wouldn't stand for one of his children not walking."

"That is so nice. You need to do it, hold your head up, and be proud of your accomplishment."

"I am trying, but soon the Social Security money will run out, and I will have to move from the apartment. I am trying to prepare for what is to come, but I honestly don't know what I am doing."

"You will have to get a job and find a place to live. Maybe you can move to California with Adam. I don't know, Angel. Everything will be so much different when I get out of here. I will do my best from this side, but there isn't a whole lot I can do."

"I will figure this out. I was raised by one of the strongest women I know. I can do it."

"I know you can. I have no doubt. I went to Church today, and it was amazing. You need to get back into Church, Angel. The Church will help you, and you need the support of good people in your life. Please start going again."

"Church in prison. That must be different."

"It wasn't. It reminded me of our little Church. Nothing fancy, just good people who are searching for the same things. I liked it a lot."

"I will see about getting a ride from the Toney's. I am sure they would pick me up. I probably need it."

"We all do. I need to go. I love you. I will call every week."

"I love you too, Mom."

I wanted so desperately to be at Angel's graduation and to hug her. It was hard to express how proud I was of her over a phone call. I wanted to talk to Adam too, but it had been months since I heard his voice. Once they locked me up, I lost all contact with him. Not because we wanted to but because he was trying to survive, and most of the time, he didn't have a telephone. I missed them both a great deal. That was the worst part about the whole situation. I missed my children. I cried for hours laying on my bed, yearning for them. Jo gave me my space as I grieved. It is a hard thing to understand when you grieve for someone who is still alive. It is a different kind of grief, one that rips your heart in two, but no one understands. Knowing that someone you love so much is within reach, but you can't touch them.

"You okay down there?" Jo asked.
"I will be. I think."
"You can talk to me if you need to."
"I am worried about my children, especially my daughter. Please don't take this the wrong way, but after you told me your story, I worry even more. You had a good life as a child, yet you ended up here. Angel's life wasn't so good, and I fear she will meet someone like Martin, who will lead her down a dreadful path. I can't do anything to stop it."
"I don't take offense to that. It is true. I could have taken a different road, but I made those choices, so here I am. I am sure your daughter will make better choices than I did, than you did, but if she doesn't, that is on her. Don't blame yourself."
"You are smart beyond your years, Jo. Thank you."
"Any time."

We laid quietly in our bunks for a half hour or so. My mind kept wandering back to Pastor Mel's message that morning.

"Hey, Jo. What is Pastor Mel's story?"
"Now that one could be a movie."
"So, you know?"

"Pastor Mel and I were cellmates when I first got here. I know a lot about her."

"Can you share?"

"She tells her story from time to time, so I guess I can."

"I am listening."

"Mel grew up in the inner city. I think she was originally from Chicago or someplace like that. Her father was a mean, mean man, but he loved Mel because she was an athlete, and people were continually complimenting him on Mel's athletic abilities. She had a couple of brothers, but none of them were as good at sports as she was. Her dad used to beat all of them regularly, except for Mel. He was severely violent to her mother, and she told me stories about how she had to stop her father from beating on the others. Of course, they all resented her because she was not a target of the abuse. Her father highly favored her, and they all knew it, which made them turn against her.

She got a full ride to play basketball at a Christian college down south. She told me that she was doing well in college and had dreams of playing overseas and doing ministry there. She didn't go home much because they couldn't afford it, but she talked to her mother on occasion and her father. Her brothers wanted nothing to do with her because they felt abandoned by her for leaving, and they still hated her for how they grew up and the special treatment she received.

Before she graduated, a local businessman bought her a plane ticket to fly home to see her family. It had been years since she had seen them. She said when she showed up; her mother was beaten up badly by her father. She said she wasn't shocked by it because it happened all her life, but something was different about that time. She thought maybe it was because she was older and had been away for so long that she felt more disgusted by it and by him. Her mother had become so submissive that she rarely even spoke for herself. This bothered Mel because she was in a place that encouraged women to be individuals and speak out against violence.

The day before she was to return to college, she walked in on her father beating her mother with a belt. She said she tried to pull him off, but she wasn't strong enough. For the first time in her life, her father struck her, and a fight ensued. She said she picked up the closest thing she could grab, which happened to be a brass candlestick, and started swinging it at her father. Before Mel knew it, she had beat her father to death. She said she partially blacked out, so she couldn't remember any details. Her father's abuse so damaged her mother that she testified in court against Mel. The man was dead because Mel was trying to protect her mother, but she turned her back on Mel, and so did her brothers.

Mel was still bitter when I got here, but she

learned to let go of her bitterness and hatred over time. That is when she got into the ministry. Now she is trying to help others like herself get through this. She is an intelligent and remarkable person, and I am thankful that she pulled me up out of the darkness."

"That is an amazing story. I knew there was something deep about Mel."

"Rachel, you will find that in this place, there are many stories just like hers, like mine. Most of the women here are not bad people; they were put in bad situations that made them react. Most of them are survivors of circumstance. They are not criminals."

Chapter 6
Mail call

I began spending most of my days with Pastor Mel and Jo. The two of them were inspiring and encouraging. We played cards, read the bible, and told stories about the old days. We were all very similar in many ways. Our lives were full of twists and turns and ultimately fatal endings.

I didn't have visitors like many of the other inmates. I spent visiting day in my cell, longing for my children and dreaming about what my life could have been. Angel graduated high school and soon after moved to Pittsburg to pursue a career in the travel industry. Just like me, she wanted to be a flight attendant and travel the world. Adam became the CEO of a large bank in California. They were both moving on with their lives and pursuing their dreams. I was happy for them both, but the distance made it impossible for visits.

On occasion, I would receive a letter from Adam or Angel with pictures of their adventures. I held those pictures close to my heart and frequently closed my eyes, imagining I was there with them. All I had was my dreams that kept me close to my children.

"Rachel, you have mail."

"Oh, good. I can't wait to see what the kids are up to." I said with excitement.

"This isn't a letter from your kids." Jo handed me an envelope.

"Who could this be from?"

"Maybe you have an admirer."

"That is doubtful." I rolled my eyes as I swiftly opened the letter.

I slowly read the two-page letter. My expression must have been of shock as Jo waiting patiently to hear who it was from.

"So, who is it from?"

"It is from Jacob."

"Who the hell is Jacob?"

"Jacob was a friend of mine and Bryan's. We met him when we moved to the mountain. He moved there shortly after we did, and we all became close friends."

"So, what does the letter say?"

"He lives in Phoenix now and wants to visit me."

"Are you going to put him on your visitor list? You don't get any visitors, Rachel."

"It just seems odd to me that he would want to visit me after all this time."

"Maybe he likes you." Jo giggled, swaying back and forth like a schoolgirl.

"Really, Jo?"

"Some people get off on that. They have some

fantasy about being with an incarcerated person. I don't understand it, but people are strange."

"He was at my sentencing hearing. I didn't know why he would be there, but I had other things to think about at the time, so I forgot about it."

"Maybe he is some minister now or something and wants to save you."

"I am not going to put him on the list. It doesn't make sense, and it is quite strange if you ask me." I threw the letter in the trash and continued with my day.

I received a letter every week from Jacob for months after that first letter, but I never responded, and I never put him on my visitor list. Jacob would send positive quotes written on note cards, and he would talk about his job as a car salesman. I began looking forward to his letters as they were the only thing I had that still connected me with the outside world. Each week Jo and I would wait for another one of Jacob's letters. Sometimes they were long funny stories, and sometimes they were just brief one or two paragraphs. He wanted desperately to visit me, but I still refused.

"Rachel, maybe you should let him come visit. Maybe he is lonely and needs a friend. Shit, he has written you every week for the last several months."

"Maybe I should. I guess it would be nice to see another face besides yours." I laughed.

47

"You know you like looking at big sexy every day. Now write that dude a letter and let him visit you."

I wrote a short letter to Jacob and told him how much Jo and I enjoyed his letters. I told him I would put him on the list to visit just this once, but not anymore after.

Visiting day was a big deal for most of the women, but today would be my first visit. I was nervous. Jo helped me fix my hair and put on makeup, which I hadn't done in a long time. It was a big day.

I reluctantly sat down at a round stainless-steel table, waiting for Jacob's arrival. One by one, visitors were reunited with their loved ones. There were many children there that day, and it warmed my heart to see some of the women I knew embracing their children and families. I was a bit jealous of their reunions, but I was happy for them too.

Jacob sat down across from me as our eyes met, and we exchanged smiles.

"It is good to see you, Rachel."

"You too, Jacob, but I still don't understand why you have been so adamant about seeing me."

"I just wanted to check on an old friend."

"Why are you here?"

"Rachel, I was on the mountain the day they found Bryan. The whole place was shocked at his death, and most of the town believed you killed him. There wasn't a thorough investigation done because they already found you guilty. I couldn't believe it. I knew you and Bryan both, and I couldn't imagine that you could do such a thing. I know you all had your issues, and yes, I knew he was abusive at times, but I didn't see it the way others saw it. I was angry that the town didn't do their part in investigating his murder."

"I didn't do it."

"I know that you didn't, and it was hard to hear that you confessed to it."

"I didn't have a choice. The prosecutor was going to bring charges on my children, and I wasn't going to let that happen."

"I guess after you confessed, I believed you did it, too, but then I heard a similar story about someone confessing unwillingly, and it sat with me for a long time."

"Why were you in court during my sentencing?"

"I had just moved to Phoenix when I heard on the radio that you were to be sentenced in Maricopa County. I did a little digging and found out the day and time. I wanted you to see a familiar face because I knew it had to be frightening and lonely."

"That is an understatement. This whole thing has been one heartbreak after another. I haven't seen my children in over two years. They sentenced me to twenty years, and not one person fought for me."

"I know. That is why I am here. When I moved to

the mountain, you and Bryan befriended me when I was very much alone. You welcomed me into your home, you fed me, and shared your lives with me. I owe it to you, Rachel, to be here now for you and to be your friend."

"I am glad we were there for you. I guess I didn't know how much that meant to you."

"I have once again found myself alone, and I thought maybe we both could use a friend."

"I know I sure can." I softly smiled.

"I enjoyed writing to you every week. I don't have any family left after my older brother passed a few years ago. Writing to you made me feel like I had a purpose."

"I have enjoyed reading your letters, too. My children can't visit because Adam is in California and Angel is in Pittsburg. They write when they can, but you know how being young is. They don't have time for much else, let alone writing a letter."

"Well, if you would like, I want to continue writing to you, and I would like to see you regularly too."

"I think that would be nice. Now that I know why you wanted to visit and that you aren't some weirdo infatuated with incarcerated women." I laughed.

"What?" Jacob looked puzzled.

"My cellmate said there are people out there that like women in prison. I don't know; she says crazy things sometimes."

"I am no weirdo, Rachel, just a friend."
"Thank you."
"Times up." The guard yelled.
"I will keep writing. Can I visit next week?"
"That would be nice. Take care, Jacob."

My visit with Jacob was refreshing. It was nice hearing him talk about how much we meant to him. I felt like my entire life was a failure, so hearing that I touched someone else's made my day.

"So, was he a weirdo?" Jo couldn't wait to hear all about my visit.
"The visit was quite nice, and no, he isn't a weirdo."
"So, he likey you?" Jo laughed.
"Shut up, Jo, you are ridiculous. Let's go eat lunch."

I now had something to look forward to each week—a visit from a friend, a change of conversation, and a feeling of acceptance. Things were looking up.

Chapter 7
The letters

I became comfortable doing my time. I made friends, Jacob was visiting me regularly, and my children sent money and letters when they could. I knew I didn't kill Bryan, but most of the women locked up didn't do the crime for which they were serving time. If they couldn't get out of their situations, I knew there was no way for me to get out of mine. I gave up on ever thinking that could be a possibility. I did what I had done all my life. I hunkered down and made the best of my circumstances.

Jo was like me; she didn't have visitors. Her parents were gone, and her sister was raising a family in Utah. Every so often, she would receive an envelope with drawings and paintings her niece and nephew drew. At the bottom of the envelope would be a brief letter from her sister.

"My sister is funny." Jo chuckled.

"Did you get another letter?"

"Yeah. My sister never says much. She is afraid to tell me that her life is great because of how mine turned out. I think she blames herself for leaving me after our parents died. I wanted to do my own thing, though. She just doesn't get it."

"I think that about my children sometimes. Their letters are reserved. They don't understand that I am living through them, and I want to hear the details."

"I know, I think the same thing about my sister. I need to tell her."

"You are always writing her; you should say something. Every time I look up at you, you are writing something. I assume they are letters to your sister."

"Yeah, mostly. I write a lot of stuff. It passes the time."

Jo was extremely smart, self-taught, but smart. She read book after book and spent hours in the library researching God only knows what. I sometimes wondered if Jo felt it was pointless. She was never getting out of prison, so; her education was useless. But every day, she marched to the library and planted her butt in a hard wooden chair, reading and studying for hours.

"You have mail, Rachel."

I jumped up. I had been anxiously awaiting my weekly letter from Jacob or one of my children, but it wasn't a letter from one of them. It was a letter from a Yolanda Washington with the Innocence Project. Who is this, and how does she even know anything about me? I thought.

Dear Mrs. Havens,

My name is Yolanda Washington, and I am with the Innocence Project of New York. I have received the hundreds of letters sent to us on your behalf. In the twenty years that I have been a part of this group, I have never received such compelling and well-written letters from someone other than the accused.

Due to the continuous letters we have received, your case has caught the eye of my associates and myself. I want to make arrangements to speak with you further about your case. My contact information is below. I look forward to hearing from you.

I held the letter for several minutes, trying to figure out who would have sent hundreds of letters. My children rarely sent me letters, let alone write hundreds to the Innocence Project. Did Jacob write these letters? My mother? Who?

"Hey, Rachel, what do you have going on today? Mel and I are going to hang out later. Do you want to come?" Jo peeked her head into our cell before returning to the library.

"Jo, did you write these letters?"

"What letters?"

"The hundreds of letters that the Innocence Project received about my case."

"Umm. I might have sent a couple of letters."

"Jo, they said they received hundreds of letters."

"That might be right. I don't keep track of that stuff."

"That means you had to have written at least twice a week for the last two years."

"Okay. I mean, I don't have anything else to do." Jo laughed.

"Seriously, Jo. Why would you do that?"

"Because you are innocent, Rachel."

"I am not getting out of here. You are just wasting your time and getting my hopes up."

"Are you mad at me?"

"No, I am not mad. I don't understand."

"Come with me. I want to show you something."

Neither of us spoke a word as we walked through the prison to the library. I had only visited the library one other time. It was large and smelt of old dusty books that had probably been donated over the years. Jo stopped abruptly in front of a tall wooden door that led to a utility closet, or so I assumed. Jo held her head down as she began to speak.

"Before I came here, I always dreamed of being a lawyer. When I was in high school, I took college classes to finish my Bachelor's in three years. I was a good student, straight A's. I planned to go onto college and later pursue that career. I wanted to be a lawyer since I was a kid; it was all I thought about.

After I came here, I was hopeless, and I knew my dream of becoming a lawyer would never be fulfilled. Even if I got out someday, I could never be a lawyer with a record. It crushed my spirit so much that at one point, I was ready to off myself.

Pastor Mel truly pulled me up out of the darkness that I was sitting in for so long. She had been doing her ministry for several years, and I attended church every Sunday, hoping I could make sense of my life. Why was I here? What was the point of my existence?

One day after church, Pastor Mel and I sat alone at a table outside. The sun was shining, and there was a cool breeze blowing; it was fall. I will never forget that conversation. I continued to talk to her about my hopelessness, and she listened. Then she grabbed my hand and said, "Jo, what are you good at? Whatever you were good at out there, you can be good at in here. You can still be whoever you dreamed about being. God has a plan for you; he has given you the tools; now you need to put them into action. Do all the good you can do, and your life will not have been in vain."

I pondered her words for a while, and then one day, I came here. I started picking up books and reading them. After a while, I noticed that every book I picked up was about law. It was my passion.

I slowly began taking books back to my cell, and before I knew it, I had hundreds of books piled up. I could quote cases, talk about statutes, and advise anything from traffic violations to murder. Women began coming to me for advice about their circumstances, and one by one, I would do my best to help them write appeals, talk to their lawyers, and fight for their freedom.

I imagine Pastor Mel got tired of the constant traffic coming and going from our cell, or maybe she just saw potential in me. I don't know, but unbeknownst to me, Mel went to the Warden on my behalf.

One day the Warden called for me. I figured I had done something wrong, and I anticipated some sort of punishment. I pled with him and promised to return all the books I had hoarded in my cell as he led me to this door. He handed me the key and said, "Go do all the good you can do." He never explained himself; he just walked away as I unlocked the door."

Jo unlocked the door and held it open as she let me look around. All four walls of that tiny room were covered with shelves full of books. Several old rusty filing cabinets sat against a window that was covered with metal bars. File boxes and manila folders full of paper cluttered the room, and a small desk with a half-empty cup of coffee sat in the middle. My eyes widened as I discovered the work that Jo had secretly been doing.

"Now you know where I spend my days. I am trying to do all the good I can do here. Rachel, I wrote those letters because you deserve to be free, and just like me, someone else made a move on my behalf. If it weren't for Mel going to the Warden, I would never have this room, and I would never be able to do what I have been doing for years to help others. Sometimes we need someone else to validate who we are to others. Make a move for us."

"This is unbelievable. I can't believe that you have been doing this, and I never knew. I really can't believe that the Warden let you do this."

"Warden Johnson is a unique person. I found out some time ago that he reads about every inmate. The Warden knows all of our stories. I am not sure about his past, but I have heard that he has seen the justice system fail many people, and that is why he became a warden. That is why he works hard to create rehabilitation programs. He, too, is trying to do all the good he can do."

"Unreal. So, you are the prison lawyer. A lot of things make sense now." I smiled at Jo.

"Yeah, and they pay me with cupcakes." We both laughed.

Chapter 8
Do All the Good You Can Do

It became clear to me that most people in that prison were trying to do good and right the wrongs they had done. I wanted desperately to find my good. They inspired me, everyone one of them from the Warden to Jo and Pastor Mel. All of them had heartbreaking stories to tell, but they used those stories to write better endings, endings that spoke of heroism, kindness, and selflessness. All of them were better than most of the people I knew on the outside. They were doing good without ever asking for anything in return. Except for cupcakes, Jo wanted cupcakes. I wanted to be more like the people inside that prison than I did the people outside. There was goodness in them, and I needed to find my good.

"Jo, how do I find my good?" Jo read quietly above me.

"What are you good at?"

"Nothing. I am not good at anything."

"Everyone is good at something, Rachel."

"I can make a pretty good pie."

"Damn, girl, you have been holding out on me. You know I like my sweets." Jo giggled.

"Making a pie isn't going to do any good in here. You are a lawyer; Mel's a preacher. I don't have those types of talents."

"You are so wrong, Rachel. All contribution is good. You must decide if that is what you want to contribute. It is that simple."

"You just want me to make pies so you can have some." I laughed.

"There is no doubt about that, but think of it like this. There are plenty of women in this prison that didn't have momma's and grand momma's teaching them how to cook. Some day one of them may get out of here, have a family, run a business, or need to find a job. You start making pies in the kitchen, and then you find others to teach how to make pies. One day when that woman is free, she may get the chance to have Thanksgiving dinner with her family and bring the best pie ever. At that moment, when her family is raving about her creation, she is going to think back to the woman who taught her how to make it. She might find herself working in a restaurant making pies, or hell, she might open a bakery because one person inspired her to do it. That is how good works. You don't have to have a lot of talent to be willing to share the talent or knowledge you have with others. Do all the good you can do."

I continued to search for my good. I still didn't think that making pies would help anyone, but maybe it would keep me busy. I spoke to the kitchen super to see if I could work there, preparing meals. Most of the workers were there as a punishment, peeling potatoes and slopping food onto trays, so they welcomed a willing volunteer. I started out doing the dishes, a job no one wanted. I then moved on to making big pots of soups and stews. After proving that I was committed to the job, I eventually asked the super if I could use some supplies to make her a pie. She gladly accepted.

"Bell, (short for Bellman, her last name) I made you an apple pie. Do you want to try it?"
"You know I do." Bell walked quickly to the prep table and leaned over to smell the warm apple pie.
"Let me cut you a piece. Some vanilla ice cream would make this pie complete. Do you know where we could score some?"
"Wait, I think I do." Bell went to the back freezer and pulled out a bucket of vanilla ice cream.
"We have some?" I said shocked.
"The Warden has a sweet tooth and occasionally comes in here searching for something. I put this on the order a couple of months back. I forgot it was in there."
"So, what do you think?"
"This is by far the best freaking pie I have ever had. Give me another piece."

Bell and I ate pie until we were sick to our stomachs. We hardly said a word as we shoveled one bite after another in our mouths. It made me feel accomplished knowing I could serve up a good piece of pie and put a smile on Bell's face.

"Rachel, you could seriously sell this shit."

"Pretty sure I can't do that in here. It is not mine to sell, but I could make pies regularly and maybe teach others how. We could have one day a week or month that we serve them as a special treat."

"Now that is a great idea. Let me talk to the Warden. We better save him a piece if we want to convince him to let us do it. I meet with him this afternoon to go over my budget. I will run it by him."

"I can't wait to see what he says. I better get back to work. Enjoy your pie." Bell held up her fork and smiled as she struggled to swallow her last bite.

I was excited to see what would come of the pie-making. Maybe Jo was right; you don't have to be a lawyer or pastor to do good.

Bell informed me that the Warden devoured his piece of apple pie and delighted in the idea of having a pie day for the women to enjoy. It was going to be a challenging task that would take much preparation and planning. I started my journey that afternoon as the prison pie maker. I needed help if it was ever going to happen. For each prisoner to have a piece of pie, I would have to make hundreds of pies each week. I couldn't do it alone.

"Jo, you are officially looking at the prison pie maker. Bell has convinced the Warden to let me make pies each week for the other women. I am going to need your help in recruiting my elves."

"That is great, Rachel. See, I told you there is good in everyone. Man, I can't wait to get my hands on a piece of that pie."

"Here, I snuck you a piece." I handed Jo a piece of apple pie that I was able to sneak from the kitchen. It was smashed in plastic wrap so I could get it out in my waistband. I don't think the appearance made much of a difference to her, though.

"Damn, girl, that is one delicious piece of pie. Let's get to work on recruiting. I am looking forward to my weekly pie now. How many women will you need to make this work?" Jo grabbed a piece of paper and started taking nots.

"Ten, twenty, I don't know. A lot, it is going to take a lot of hands to make this work."

"I will start putting the word out today. How about I make a deal with you."

"What kind of deal." Jo was always making deals.

"Those pre-packaged cupcakes I get for payment of my services do not hold a candle to this pie. If I can get you the workers you need and you pull this off, I want payment in pies."

"That is a deal." Jo and I shook on it. We were now in the pie-making business together.

Jo knew many women in that prison. She had

provided her services for them throughout her time there. Some of them were indebted to her for various reasons, so she called on all the owed favors. Recruiting over twenty women to help me make this pie thing a reality.

For several weeks I spent every day teaching other women how to make a crust from scratch and flavor a pie with just the right ingredients. Our pies were the talk of the prison. Everyone wanted to get their hands on a piece of homemade pie.

We were able to make one hundred pies for our first big pie reveal. One hundred pies were not enough for every woman to get a piece, which meant they needed to arrive early to chow if they wanted a chance at a piece of pie. It was a big day for me. I had fed my family for years, made pies for family gatherings, and offered them to sick neighbors, but this was a memorable day. The women's faces enjoying various pies and reminiscing about holidays and family dinners brought so much joy to me. I had done good.

Chapter 9
If All Else Fails, Eat Pie

My mother had spoken to me years ago about how a cake was comfort. When you feel sad or when you are celebrating, a cake is a way of expression. She spoke about how life was like cake. There are tasteless ingredients, and then there are sweet ones. Combine them, and you have a delicious cake. Life, the not-so-good parts, and the great parts are combined to make what we call life. I finally got what she had said to me all those years ago. It takes both sadness and happiness, pain and joy, rejoicing and heartbreak to make up a life. It is how you look at it that determines if it is a good life or a bad life.

At the beginning of my journey, Jo told me that I could have a decent life here if I wanted to. She was right. I had become something that would have never been possible on the outside. I was a well-known baker in here, praised by the other women. Outside of here, I was just Rachel, and most people never gave me a second thought. I was becoming comfortable in my role, and honestly, I wasn't sure that I wanted out. Other than seeing my children, this place had become something to me. It was home.

Each morning I woke up and started my day by instructing several women on our pie plan. We served pies once a month, so it was essential to make them, freeze them and have them ready for our monthly pie day. It was a celebration day of sorts. Women started coming to me asking to help. Many of them wanted to be a part of it because it had turned into an excellent experience for those involved. They, too, were celebrated by the other women. They received praise for their hard work and delicious pies.

One afternoon I was approached by a young lady. I had seen her before, but I couldn't recall our encounter.

"Are you Rachel?"
"Yes, how can I help you."
"I was hoping I could help you with the pies."
"Do I know you? You look familiar."
"I don't know." The girl gently smiled.
"Yes, I do know you. You came here the same time I did. You were in the van with me when we arrived."
"Oh, yeah. I was. I remember you now."
"Do you know anything about baking?"
"No. I used to watch my grandma make pies when I was a child, but I have never made one myself."
"Come back at 7 am sharp. Be ready to work and learn."
"I will be here. Thank you."

The young girl still seemed lost. I recalled my encounter with her in the van. She reminded me so much of Angel and my heart ached to see such a young girl going to prison. I wanted to give her an opportunity to start living again. Maybe this could be the open door for her to find her way in this place. I was surprised to see her waiting for me as I arrived the next morning. She seemed determined to be a part of this adventure, and I was glad to have her join me.

"So, what is your name, kiddo?" I said as we walked into the kitchen.
"My name is Tori."
"Where are you from, Tori?"
"Wisconsin."
"Well, I am glad to have you. Put an apron on, and we will get started."

Tori and I spent several hours together as I guided her through the process of making a pie. We talked and exchanged stories. She would become my project, and I would mentor her just like Jo had done with me. I was happy to have the opportunity.

"So, what got you in here, Tori?"
"I don't want to talk about it."
"Come sit down while we wait for the pies to bake." We put the pies in the oven and pulled a couple of stools up to the counter.
"I am a terrible person. If I told you what I did, you would never want to speak to me again."

"I can't imagine that. We are in prison, and there are many unspeakable things that women in here have done. You can't take it back, whatever it was, but you also can't keep it bound up. It would help if you talked about it, to heal from it. Walk back through the pain so you can move on and begin the healing process."

Tori hung her head as tears flowed down her smooth pale cheek. She was so young, and I could not imagine her doing anything so horrible that she would be sitting in prison. I put my hand on her shoulder and did my best to comfort her.

"I killed my son." Tori began sobbing uncontrollably.

"What happened?" I teared up as I watched her heartbreak.

"Dillon was born prematurely. He was only three pounds when he was born, but he was beautiful. I had never seen anything so amazing in my life. He was in the children's hospital for several months. I practically lived there with him. It was hard. He had a lot of problems because he was born early. He was deaf and would probably have been autistic if he had lived longer, but I will never know.

I suffered from depression all my life. My mother put me on medicine, but nothing seemed to work. I couldn't get out of bed for days at a time, even as a child. When I got pregnant with Dillon, I was determined to figure it out and be the best mom I could be, but I wasn't well. The doctor put me on an antidepressant after he was born so I could function. Having a child in the hospital was exhausting, scary, and frustrating. The medicine worked for a little while, but it gave me severe mood swings. I felt like a crazy person; there were these high, highs and low, lows. I couldn't get it under control.

Eventually, Dillon was able to come home. He was better, but he was still sick. I didn't know what to do with a sick child. I didn't have the nurses around helping me as they did in the hospital. I was overwhelmed. He woke me up in the middle of the night one-night screaming. I couldn't make him stop. Nothing I did comforted him. I fed him, changed him, and rocked him, but he continued to scream for hours. I don't know what happened. I guess I snapped. I put a pillow over his face as he screamed until he stopped crying. Before I knew it, I had suffocated him. I killed my child. That is the most unspeakable crime there could ever be. Before I went on trial, they diagnosed me with bipolar and personality disorder. My attorney wanted to use it as a defense in my case, but I didn't care. I deserved every bit of punishment handed down to me."

"I can't imagine what you are going through. Mental illness is real and is trial and error until they find something that works for you. You can't blame yourself. We need more studies done and more help for those suffering. You are not alone Tori, thousands of people suffer from it."

"Maybe, but they don't kill their children."

"My mom used to drag me to the kitchen to eat cake when life seemed like not worth living. It was her way of showing she cared. I don't have any cake, but I do have pie. I can't make the pain go away, but I can share a piece of pie with you, so you know that I care about you, and I am here for you. When all else fails, eat pie."

Chapter 10
The Innocence Project

I kept Tori close to me. I now felt a sense of responsibility for her since I was the only person she had shared her story with. She was a child, just like my children, and she needed someone to look after her, and I wanted to be that person. I wanted to give her hope, that same hope Jo had so graciously given to me.

I buried myself in my work as the prison pie maker. I continued to see Jacob regularly and talk to my children on occasion. Time was flying by, but I still had a long way to go. Jo continued to bug me about the letter I received from the Innocence Project. She wanted me to reach out to Yolanda Washington and at least get a feel for what she might be able to do for me. I still wanted my freedom, but I had become comfortable with my life in prison. I was torn between my life in here and my life out there.

"When are you going to respond to the Innocence Project?" Jo asked.

"I have thought about it, but honestly, Jo, I am getting comfortable living with you in here. Plus, I don't think it will make a difference. I don't want to waste their time."

"That is what they do, Rachel. They help people

like you fight your case. You need to call her and give it a chance. I like you being my celly, but you deserve to get out of here and live a good life."

"I am living a good life. I am making a difference in here."

"Yes, you are, but you can make a difference out there too. Don't you want to see your children?"

"Of course, I do. You know I miss my children dearly."

"Then make the call, Rachel."

Jo had been my voice of reason for several years. She always knew what to say to make me think about my actions and my choices. I continued to ignore her nagging about the Innocence Project until I received a letter from Angel.

Angel was twenty years old now and just discovered that she was pregnant. I was overjoyed at the thought of being a grandmother, but I couldn't be a grandmother from prison. It was time to do something.

"Yolanda Washington speaking."

"Ms. Washington, my name is Rachel Havens. You reached out to me some time back about my case. I think I am ready to meet with you."

"I have been expecting your call. I didn't think it would take this long, but I would like to discuss your case further. I can arrange for a flight out to see you early next week."

"That would be great. Is there anything I need to do to prepare for our meeting?"

"No. I have your case file. I requested it months ago. I have just been waiting to hear from you."

"I look forward to our meeting. Thank you."

"See you soon."

I anxiously waited for my initial meeting with Ms. Washington. I was nervous but hopeful. It had been a couple of years since I spoke about what happened and why I ended up here. I knew I would have to replay the incident to her, and I was not looking forward to reliving those memories.

Ms. Washington would now be my official lawyer, and she would be able to visit with me as much as and whenever she wanted. I didn't have to reserve my visiting hours for her. She arrived on a Wednesday afternoon. When the guard called for me, my stomach began to turn. I knew I would soon be rehashing my past.

"Hello, Rachel. I am glad that you decided to reach out. Your cellmate must think a great deal of you to have sent all those letters. It was hard to ignore."

"I can imagine. Jo is a wonderful person, and I am lucky to have her."

"So, let's get started. I have reviewed your case and what I can't figure out is why you confessed to murder if you didn't do it."

"When they arrested me, I didn't even know that my husband had been killed. I found out the next day when the public defender, Mr. Andrews, told me. They assumed I did it because I left Arizona and went back to Indiana, where I am from originally. I left because I was tired of being abused by him and I had enough. Everyone thought I did it because we had a huge fight the night before, and many people witnessed it. I didn't kill him, though."

"That is why I am here. What was said to you that made you confess?"

"Mr. Andrews said that if I didn't confess, they were going to bring charges on my children. My son was 18, and my daughter 16 at the time. He said the prosecutor thought they helped me. I had no other choice. I couldn't let them put my children through that."

"That makes more sense to me now. This happens a lot in situations like this. It is a tactic that is used quite often to get people to confess. Even though Mr. Andrews was supposed to be helping you, he was helping those that he ultimately worked for. A confession saves thousands of dollars because they can forgo a trial and all the resources they need to prove your guilt. They use tricks like that when a person is at their weakest. They are in jail, scared and unsure. That is why I do what I do, Rachel. It is not justice, and we are going to get to the bottom of it. I will be spending a great deal of time trying to unravel the reasons behind them forcing you into a confession. I need to know the names of people who might have witnessed your fight with your husband. Also, anyone that might have seen the abuse over the years. I will be meeting with Mr. Andrews at some point to see what his thinking was at that moment. Can you get all that information together for me?"

"Yes, of course. That is one thing that didn't seem fair about the whole situation. Mr. Andrews let me record my confession and told me that they would reduce my charges to manslaughter because of my confession. When I arrived in Arizona for my sentencing, there was no recorded confession, and they charged me with second-degree murder. He didn't fight for me like he said he would. No one heard the recorded confession where I spoke about the abuse. I told Mr. Andrews I didn't kill my husband, and he said he believed me, but it was how the justice system works."

"He said that he believed you were innocent?"

"Yes, but I can't prove it. Mr. Andrews had already turned off the recorder."

"Rachel, I have been doing this for a many years. It has been my life's work. This kind of injustice happens all of the time. Unfortunately, it happens to people more often in small towns and people who do not have the means to fight it. We will fight this."

"Thank you. Ms. Washington, do you mind me asking why you do this work?"

Ms. Washington took a deep breath and fiddled with her pen before she began to speak.

"When I was a freshman in high school, my older brother was arrested for a crime that happened in our neighborhood. He was nineteen years old. My family knew that he didn't commit the crime because he was home with us when the crime happened, but they had already found him guilty before an investigation was ever done. My family didn't have the money for an attorney. So, just like you, we had to rely on the public defender to represent my brother. He was found guilty and sentenced to death. Just before his twenty-fifth birthday, they executed him. A few years later, they discovered through DNA that my brother didn't commit the crime. It was too late.

So, I decided to go to college and become a lawyer that would fight the justice system. I would only take on cases that I believed the convicted was innocent. I passed up many opportunities over the years, but I held true to my decision. I would spend my life honoring my brother and others like him.

After ten or so years, I was approached by the Innocence Project. It is everything I believe in and fight for. It is what I was called to do. Don't worry, Rachel, you are in good hands."

"I believe I am. Thank you, Ms. Washington."

"Call me Yolanda. I will be in touch."

Yolanda winked at me as she picked up her briefcase and exited the meeting room. I began to feel hopeful again. I felt as if someone was truly fighting for me and that maybe I had a chance of getting out.

Chapter 11
Touched by An Angel

I was overwhelmed by the kindness that had been shown to me. Each person I met seemed to want to help me in some way. Yolanda was an angel for what she was doing to help the innocent. Not just me but all the many people who were wrongly convicted. She knew too well that the justice system failed us. She used the tragic death of her brother to do right by others. I didn't know how much, but soon I would know how indebted I would be to her.

I couldn't wait to tell Jacob about my meeting with Yolanda. Jacob and I had become close friends through our visits and letters. I shared everything with him, and if I was on the outside, I could almost see myself having a life with him. That might be closer than I thought. I knew it would take years to fight my case, but there was hope, and I had a true hero on my side.

"Hi. How are you?"

"I am so good. You have no idea how good I am right now."

"The pie-making business is going well; I take it."

"It is but, I met with a lady this week from the Innocence Project. She is going to help me fight my case."

"That is great, Rachel. How did this come about?"

"Jo has been writing them letters for years. I was hesitant at first, but now that I am going to be a grandmother, I have to get out of here."

"You are going to be a grandmother?"

"Yes. Hadn't I told you? Angel is having a baby."

"How wonderful, Rachel. That is great. I am happy for you."

"I know I won't get out before the baby is born, but maybe I can get out before the baby gets old enough to know that I have been in prison."

"Aren't you a little concerned about opening the case?"

"Why would I be concerned?"

"What if they discover one of your children killed Bryan? You could be replacing your life for theirs."

"No way. There is no way one of them did it."

"But, what if they did? Rachel, you need to think about that."

"I thought you would be happy for me."

"I am happy for you. I want you to prepare for what could be uncovered."

"I am confident that neither of them could have done it. I am going with that."

"Okay, I will leave it alone. I am your friend. You know that. I didn't mean to upset you."

"Just drop it. What have you been up to? You didn't write or visit last week. Was there something wrong?"

"Rachel, I need to confess something to you."

"I am listening."

"I have been struggling for years with alcohol. I have been to rehab several times, but sometimes I relapse and go on a few days drunk. Last week was a bad week for me."

"I am sorry, Jacob. I didn't know you were going through that. I wish I could be there for you. Maybe I will get out soon, and I can help you."

"Thank you, but I am fighting demons that I don't think you could ever understand."

"I have plenty of demons myself. I understand more than you think. I have struggled with drugs and alcohol in the past, and I know why people do it. It is an escape from reality. I get it."

"I am getting a handle on it. Our friendship has helped me a great deal." Jacob grabbed my hand.

"I am glad. It would help if you talked to someone, though. A professional."

"I have before, but it never did any good. Those professionals don't get what I have been through."

"I will pray for you, Jacob. I don't like to see someone I care about suffer."

"Thanks, but it will take more than your prayers to fix me." Jacob chuckled.

"I missed you last week. Stay sober so you can come to visit me. Okay?"

"I will do my best. I will see you next week."

"Promise?"

"I promise."

I was genuinely concerned for Jacob, and I felt terrible that he was suffering while I was rejoicing about multiple things in my life. I couldn't help him from inside those walls, and it was even more reason for me to want to get out.

Yolanda was working diligently on my case, talking with me every week to update me on her progress. Jacob's comment about my children unsettled me. What if, by chance, one of them had something to do with Bryan's murder? Me getting out would mean one of them would be going to prison. I would never be able to live with myself if that happened.

"Hello, Rachel. I have some interesting news about your case." Yolanda said excitedly.

"I don't want to do this," I said abruptly.

"What do you mean you don't want to do this? Rachel, you are innocent, and I can get you out."

"I don't want out."

"Rachel, what is going on?"

"What if you discover one of my children killed Bryan? They will go to prison. I am not going to take that risk."

"Rachel, did either of your children own a gun?"

"No. My children weren't old enough to own a gun."

"Then they didn't kill Bryan."

"What do you mean?"

"When you confessed, you told Mr. Andrews that you shot Bryan with a 9mm handgun. Correct?"

"Yes, because that was the only gun we owned."

"You also told him that you shot Bryan two times as you held two pillows to his head. Correct?"

"Yes, because I just made it up."

"Bryan was not shot in the head; he was not shot twice, and it wasn't a 9mm."

"How do you know all of this."

"I received the autopsy report yesterday. Bryan was shot once in the chest at a distance with a 45 handgun. Your confession is all wrong. If you killed him, you would have known details. They never checked the autopsy because they did not need to after they convinced a confession out of you. Rachel, this is your out."

"Oh my God. You are an angel, Yolanda."

"I have some work to do. I must write some reports about my discovery, and then I will work on an appeal. This evidence should be all we need. Rachel, you must know that this all takes some time. An appeal is not going to happen overnight, but I think we can build a solid case. Just hold on."

"I can do that. I never thought it would be possible for me to get out of here. It is possible, isn't it?"

"You will get out. Trust me."

"Thank you, thank you."

"I will be in touch."

I couldn't wait to tell Jo about the discovery Yolanda made. I rushed back to my cell after hanging up the phone. All Jo's hard work paid off. She, too, was an angel for writing all those letters. I would never be able to repay her for her kindness.

"Jo, you are never going to believe what Yolanda just told me."

"What, that you are innocent and getting out of here. I already knew that." Jo said sarcastically.

"Jo, I am serious. My confession doesn't line up with Bryan's murder. They never checked the autopsy. They closed the case before it was open because I confessed. I am getting out."

I attempted to show my gratitude to Jo by wrapping my arms around her.

"Okay, now that is enough. You know I don't like to be touched." Jo smiled.

"Jo, how do I ever repay you for what you did by writing those letters?"

"Bake me some damn pies before you get out of here." We both laughed.

"If I get out of here, I am opening a whole bakery for you, Jo."

Chapter 12
Mr. Andrews

Yolanda moved forward with the appeal process, but she struggled to convince Mr. Andrews to meet with her about my case. She told him nothing about the autopsy, only that she was representing me and needed to speak to him regarding the matter.

We soon found out that Mr. Andrews was running for the superior court's judge, and his hesitancy was due to his run for that seat. I believe he knew from the beginning that he did wrong by me and feared the backlash he would take because of it.

Yolanda was finally able to schedule a meeting with him after she threatened to go to the local papers and tell them about the part he played in my wrongful conviction. Mr. Andrews had no idea what he was up against or who was in the ring fighting for me. Yolanda was a pit bull when it came to representing the innocent. She sunk her teeth in and didn't let up until she won the fight.

"Mr. Andrews, thank you for agreeing to meet with me. We have a lot of things to discuss."

"I am a little pressed for time, so we need to make it brief."

"Mr. Andrews, I am going to suggest that you clear your schedule for the rest of the afternoon. This meeting is going to take a while. Your career will be on the line if you don't assist me in this matter."

"Are you threatening me, Ms. Washington?"

"I am not. I will present to you the facts, and those facts will prove that you failed to do your job as a public defender in my client's case. If the word gets out, you will be finished."

"Nancy, clear my schedule for the afternoon." Mr. Andrews called to his assistant.

"Mr. Andrews, my client spoke about a recorded confession that you took a week or so after her arrest. Do you still have that recording?"

"Please call me Pete. I think I do in an old briefcase."

"I would like to hear the confession. Can you locate the old briefcase?"

"What is the big deal about that. Mrs. Havens just rambled on about her life with her husband and how he abused her."

"Is that why you re-wrote her confession to state that she killed Mr. Havens and how she killed him?"

"I didn't want to give her false hope that a judge would listen to the recorded confession."

"Did you read the confession that you wrote to Mrs. Havens?"

"No, she could have read it."

"But she didn't because you made her believe that it was a formality. She didn't know until she was sentenced in Arizona on 2nd-degree murder that you didn't share her recorded confession with anyone. She trusted you as her lawyer and thought you were doing what was best for her. Is that not true?"

"Why are you acting like I am on trial here?"

"You are, and you will be if you don't help me get Mrs. Havens out of prison."

"How am I supposed to do that?"

"Start by finding that recording."

"Here. Here it is. See for yourself; Mrs. Havens just rambles on. You can have the tape. I have no use for it."

"I will take it. Thank you. "Pete, I have spoken with the local police agency in Pinetop. The investigation into Mr. Haven's death was brief because they believed my client killed him from the beginning due to a fight they had the night before. Is it true that after my client was arrested, you spoke to the same local police agency, and they told you that without a doubt they believed Mrs. Havens killed her husband?"

"Yes. I believe it was something like that."

"At any point did you ask to see their investigation and how they came to that conclusion?"

"No. I did not."

"Did you at any point ask for documents, talk to witnesses or do an investigation of your own?"

"No. I did not. Where are you going with this, Ms. Washington?"

"As a public defender, it is your job to defend your client in their case. Is that correct?"

"Yes."

"Do you feel as if you defended Mrs. Havens?"

"She confessed. There was nothing to defend."

"Why did she confess, Mr. Andrews?"

"Because she committed the murder. Again, please call me Pete."

"Pete, is it not true that you told my client that the prosecutor was going to bring charges on her children if she didn't confess?"

"That is true. I did tell Mrs. Havens that."

"Was the prosecutor going to bring charges on her children?"

"No. I read somewhere that there are different ways to get someone to confess, which that was one of those ways. I thought I would try it, but I didn't think it would work.? I was just as surprised as anyone that she immediately confessed."

"So, let me recap. You were my client's court-appointed lawyer who was supposed to do what was in her best interest. The prosecutor never told you he would bring charges on her children, yet you told her he was to coerce a confession out of her. You never asked for the autopsy or any documentation on the investigation, and you never did any investigating yourself. Do I have all of that correct?"

"Yes, but she confessed. What are you not getting about that?"

"Mr. Andrews. I am sorry, Pete. I hold in my hand a copy of the autopsy. If you had taken the time to acquire a copy, you would know that Mrs. Haven's confession didn't line up with what happened to her husband." Ms. Washington handed Mr. Andrews a copy of the autopsy.

"As you will see, what she said in her confession is not what happened to Mr. Havens. It is all there in black and white."

"I can read." Mr. Andrews grabs the autopsy.

"If you would have acquired the autopsy and read it, Pete, you would have known that she made up her confession."

"I don't know what to say."

"Also, my client said that she told you she didn't kill her husband, and you said you knew she didn't but that it was just how the justice system works."

"It is how it works when you confess."

"You mean when you coerce a confession out of someone by threatening to bring charges on their children?"

"Ms. Washington, what do you want me to do? What is done is done."

"An innocent woman has been sitting in prison for almost four years. I want you to help me get her out."

"I can't do that."

"Why can't you?"

"If I admit to all of this, I will not win the election, and my career could be over."

"If you do nothing, I will make damn sure that your career is over. I will give you a week to think about how you are going to right the wrong you have done to Mrs. Havens."

"After a week, then what?"

"If you choose not to help me, then I will do what I need to do to burry you and your precious career."

"The election is in three weeks; can't you wait until it is over?"

"You have one week, Mr. Andrews. Good day."

Yolanda left Mr. Andrew's office, knowing she had him backed into a corner. She was going to force him one way or another to help get me out of prison. Yolanda had an evening flight, so in the meantime, she visited a local eatery and listened to my confession tape. Her eyes welled up as she heard the desperation in my voice. She was moved by my confession and all I spoke about. She knew she was doing the right thing, and there was no doubt I was innocent. She listened to the end and then rewound the tape and listened to the tape again.

"I will be damned." She said, relieved.

Chapter 13
The Confession Tape

Yolanda held in her hand my confession tape, proof that a recorded version was created. It was also proof that Mr. Andrews was only appeasing my request when he agreed to let me record it. I didn't know it at the time, but that confession tape would be my ticket out of prison. My attempt to tell my story for a lesser sentence would ultimately be the trap that would prove I did not receive proper representation.

I attempted to be patient as Yolanda worked on my case. I told everyone I was getting out. My children were delighted and were making concessions in their lives to make room for me to be home. Jacob spoke about the possibility of expanding on our friendship and having a life together. When I get released, I would have choices, and I was beginning to see those opportunities instead of thinking they were no longer reality. Jo and Tori were not looking forward to the day when I would no longer be a part of their lives. Jo had been my most trusted friend from the moment I arrived, and Tori had become my understudy, who was blossoming into a wonderful pie maker. We were family in that place, and leaving them would mean I would be leaving another family. I was excited but sad.

Yolanda made sure she secured my confession tape. Mr. Andrews was unaware that the tape would force his hand in helping me get out.

"Hi, Rachel."

"How was your meeting with Mr. Andrews?"

"He is running for judge, so he is hesitant about helping us get you out. He has no idea who he is up against."

"I am glad you are on my side." I chuckled.

"Rachel, I have your confession tape. Mr. Andrews didn't seem to think he needed it any longer."

"Of course not. He didn't use it the first time."

"I have listened to it several times. I understand why you wanted it heard. I am not sure that it would have done any good at that time, but now it will."

"How is that?"

"You thought Mr. Andrews turned the tape recorder off after your confession. He did not. The entire conversation is on that tape, included where Mr. Andrews said he believed you were innocent. I don't believe he ever listened to the tape after that day. He knew all along his plans. Once the appeals court hears the tape, you will be granted an appeal. They have no other choice. You never received fair representation."

"That is great, Yolanda."

"I still have work to do, but it is all coming together."

"Thank you for everything."
"I will call next week if I have any new information."
"I will talk to you then."

Each time I spoke to Yolanda, she seemed to have more information. Information that I didn't know about. The entire investigation was all news to me as well. I wanted to know who killed Bryan, not because I knew I didn't, but because he deserved that much. He might have been abusive to me over the years, and our marriage was rocky, but I loved him. I knew a side of Bryan that most didn't know. The side that had been overpowered by grief for years. I knew the demons he battled and the struggles he had after Tank's death. At one time, he was good to me, and we were in love. I wanted to find his killer as much as the next person, and selfishly I wanted out of prison.

I anxiously awaited to hear the confession tape I had recorded years prior. I briefly remembered what I said on the tape, but I felt crazy thinking that Mr. Andrews believed I was innocent. I thought maybe I imagined it, but the tape would prove that my imagination wasn't playing tricks on me. He did say those things, and perhaps at that moment, he believed me; nonetheless, he still proceeded with ruining my life instead of helping me. I wanted him to pay for the injustice he had done to me and probably had done to others.

"Mr. Andrews, a Ms. Yolanda Washington is on the phone for you." Nancy peeked her head in the door of Mr. Andrews's office.

"Tell her I am unavailable."

"She said it is important."

"Okay, send it through to me." He sighed.

"Hello, Ms. Washington, how can I help you?"

"It has been a week, Pete. Thought I would remind you of my demand."

"I am in the middle of an election. I can't possibly do anything to help you with your client."

"I thought you might say that."

"I would like to help you, but soon I will be a judge, and you can't go around making demands to judges."

"You will not be a judge once I contact the local paper and the news. Thank you for your time."

"Wait, wait. I don't know what I am supposed to do."

"You can first start by writing a letter to the appellate court stating your misconduct with Mrs. Havens case."

"You are asking me to make a statement in writing that I failed to do my job?"

"Exactly. You did, in fact, fail to do your job, Pete, and I have proof in my hand that you did."

"You don't have any proof. Mrs. Havens confessed. I did my job."

"Mr. Andrews, I am sorry, Pete. The tape that you handed over to me proves that you failed to give my client proper representation."

"That tape proves nothing. Mrs. Havens thought she would get a lighter sentence for expressing the grief that her husband put her through. She ultimately gave a reason to kill him."

"I see that I am at a dead end with you. I will not continue to bother you with the matter. Good day, Pete."

Yolanda knew how to play with the minds of lawyers. She had been one for a long time and had fought many cases like mine. She knew if she gave Mr. Andrews enough time to ponder her statement that he would contact her. She waited for a few days, and without fail, he called.

"Yolanda speaking."

"Ms. Washington, it is Pete Andrews. I want to sit down face to face and discuss your client."

"I thought you might."

"I only have a day or two open next week. I can fly to New York to see you."

"I will clear my schedule for a meeting. When can you be here?"

"Next Thursday."

"I will be awaiting your arrival."

As planned, Mr. Andrews showed up Thursday morning to Yolanda's office. He was prepared to plead with her about dismissing him from any plan to help in my case. Yolanda had other plans, and the confession tape was about to be the main component.

"Pete, I am glad you agreed to meet with me. What is on your mind?"

"I have a few questions about our last conversation that I need to be clarified. You said that the confession tape would prove that I didn't do my job. How so?"

"Pete, I don't believe you ever listened to the tape after that day."

"No, I didn't. I had a rough night the night before, but I remembered what she said, and so that is how I wrote the confession that she signed."

"You should have listened to the tape."

"I heard it firsthand. Why would I need to listen to it?"

"At the end of the tape, Mrs. Havens told you that she didn't kill her husband, but if you needed a confession to save her children, there was her confession. You didn't deny it. In fact, you told her that you believed she was innocent. You never turned the recorder off when you thought you did. I have the tape and the proof that you failed my client."

"I don't know what to say."

"Start by saying you plan to help me get Mrs. Havens out of prison."

Mr. Andrews hung his head, and a somberness came over him.

"Pete, are you okay?"

"Ms. Washington, I need to tell you something. It has weighed on me pretty heavy."

"I have cleared my whole day. Go ahead and say what you need to say."

"I couldn't listen to the tape again. Mrs. Havens was like looking into the eyes of my mother. My father abused my mother for years when I was a child, but I looked up to him. He was my hero, just like many sons look up to their fathers. My mother had him thrown in jail when I was around ten years old. He was gone for five years, and I hated her for sending my father away. I needed him. I was a boy, and a boy needs his father.

After he got out of jail, I went and lived with him. I never spoke to my mother again because I was furious about the time I missed with my father. A few years later, my mother fell ill with cancer that ultimately took her life. I never told her why I hated her, I never visited her when she was sick, and I never forgave myself for abandoning her and treating her that way. It wasn't long after she passed that my father re-married. He was abusive to his new wife too. All those years, I looked up to him and regarded him as a superhero, but he was nothing more than a wife beater. How hurtful that must have been for my mother to see how much I adored him, knowing how he treated her.

Mrs. Havens words hurt me deeply. My mother never told me how much my father hurt her because she knew I would never listen. I almost felt as if my mother spoke through Mrs. Havens to me that day, and it tormented me. As soon as I left Mrs. Havens, I stuffed my briefcase in the closet with the recorder inside and never pulled it back out. I didn't want to hear it ever again. I did not intend to harm Mrs. Havens. I was a young public defender with a family, and I tried to do everything I could to move up. Trust me when I tell you that I have never forgotten her or what I did. Ms. Washington, I need this position as a judge. My family is counting on me to provide and do right by them. I can't throw everything I have worked for away. There has to be another way I can help you with this."

"Don't think for a second that your story will make me have sympathy for you. A woman is sitting in prison because you didn't properly do your job and help her. She has missed out on so much of her own children's lives, so don't think that I feel sorry for you. I will say that I am glad you told me and that you are not some heartless asshole that I will despise the rest of my life. We have work to do, and if you become a judge, we will use your position in our favor to help Mrs. Havens rightfully get out of prison."

"How will we do that?"

"We are going to find the real killer, but first, I need to get her appeal going so that we can get a new trial. I will be calling on you, Pete; you can guarantee that."

"I will do what I can. I want to do this for my mother, too. Her only son wrongly convicted her, and that must have been one hell of a prison."

"We will make this right for them both. I will be in touch. Thank you for coming today. Safe travels."

"Good day, Ms. Washington."

"Call me Yolanda."

Chapter 14
Rainbow Lake

The process for getting an appeal is long. I imagine documents sit on someone's desk for months, getting shuffled around from one corner to the other. I began to lose hope even though I knew Yolanda was working hard on my case. She had others, though, and my case at times was pushed to the back burner. Yolanda knew that she would need to uncover more information and possibly discover Bryan's real killer for me to obtain a new trial and win. She was not an investigator, nor was she trained in forensics. She needed to find the best people for the job, and that would take time.

Yolanda contacted several investigators on the mountain where Bryan was killed. She flew out to meet several people she would call on from time to time, acquiring information about the case. She convinced one of them to request the case be re-opened and investigated thoroughly after revealing my confession tape. Although many people thought I killed Bryan before I confessed, it was hard to deny that I was coerced into confessing after listening to the tape.

An officer we called Pixie had become friends with Bryan during our time living in Pinetop. She was now a detective and the only female on their force.

She wanted to find Bryan's killer too. She was his friend, but she was also a hard nose policewoman who was highly respected. She jumped at the opportunity to find Bryan's killer.

As Pixie began backtracking the night before Bryans' murder, she started to uncover a dark side to Bryan that she didn't know. Many people came forward, speaking out about the abuse they witnessed and the bruises they saw on me. She uncovered an addiction problem that Bryan had and the reason for the constant financial struggle. She also contacted my children to hear their side of the story. She realized that she never knew Bryan completely, only a side that most people saw. The good side.

Pinetop is highly populated with pine trees and butts up to the Navajo Indian Reservation. There are many places a murderer could escape to without being detected. It would be a considerable undertaking for Pixie and Yolanda because there were no fingerprints taken, there was no evidence recovered, and there were no witnesses. Whoever killed Bryan was most likely going to get away with it, and I would continue to pay for his murder. Unfortunately, in these situations, you are guilty until proven innocent. That was exactly what they needed to do was prove I was innocent and that someone else killed Bryan.

Pixie was an avid mountain biker. She spent hours

amongst those tall pine trees riding her bike. She often rested and took small strolls through the woods, hoping to someday come across something that would link back to a crime. In her experience, people often found the easiest routes to disposing of evidence. The trails through those wooded areas had been a dropping ground in the past for such evidence. She hoped that it, too, would lead to some evidence in Bryan's murder.

After several months of investigating, Pixie ran into one dead end after another. She believed that whoever murdered Bryan knew him and knew me. The timing was too perfect and easily pinned on me. Whoever the murderer was, they knew our relationship, and they knew our moves. They took the opportunity that night, knowing that all fingers would be pointed towards me. They would get away with murder, and I would take the fall for it.

Who, though? Who would want to kill Bryan intentionally? Most people knew him to be a kind person, a talented musician, and a fun-loving guy. He had no known enemies and never hurt anyone except for me. I once again became the prime suspect; proving I didn't kill him would be difficult.

"Hello, Yolanda, it's Pixie."
"I am hoping you have some good news for me."
"Unfortunately, I don't. Every road leads to Rachel. She is the only one who had reason to kill Bryan."
"She didn't kill him. I have been doing this a long

time, and I know she didn't kill him."

"Has she ever given any indication of who might have wanted Bryan dead? I am not finding anyone. Most people liked him for the most part."

"The only thing that she mentioned, in the beginning, was that she was afraid that we might uncover that one of her children did it."

"I don't know about that. There wasn't a thorough investigation done, but whoever did it had a plan in place. I don't believe Mrs. Haven's children were mature enough to plan like that. If they killed him, it would have been at the spur of the moment and not thought out. They couldn't have covered their tracks that easily. I think one of them would have given in by now, overcome with guilt."

"I was hoping this would be easier than it has been. I am starting to lose hope. Thank you, Pixie, for all that you are doing on your end."

"I want to figure this out too. This has been one of the most challenging cases I have ever worked on. I will keep searching, but for now, it looks like Rachel is staying in prison."

Pixie stopped her investigation for a while. She had to focus on other cases she had on her plate, and the roads to Bryan's murder were leading nowhere.

While on vacation in California, Pixie received a phone call from a fellow detective. She quickly cut her vacation short when she learned that a gun was recovered from Rainbow Lake.

Rainbow Lake, a small lake that Bryan and Angel often fished when we lived on the mountain. It was a clean lake and full of tasty fish. It was also easily accessed and visited by many tourists and locals. It was the perfect spot to dispose of evidence quickly.

"Pixie, I am glad you are back, but there was no need to cut your vacation short." Her fellow detective said.

"What have you found?"

"It's a 45. Of course, there is some damage from the water, but the serial numbers are clear, and we could possible get ballistics from it."

"I want a bullet comparison done immediately. Once the gun is dry, we need to fire a round or two."

"I have already made arrangements with the lab in Phoenix. I have had our firearms expert look the gun over, and he believes it is ready to fire a couple of shots."

"Let's do it then. I want to find out if this is the gun used in Bryan's murder. We may finally have a lead."

Pixie and her associate took steps to acquire a couple of bullets from the 45-handgun found in Rainbow Lake. They sent them off to the lab along with the bullet recovered from Bryan's body during his autopsy. There was a slight bit of hope that this could be the weapon that would lead to Bryan's killer. The tests could take months, and finding who the gun belonged to could take longer. Guns are often bought on the open market with no record to the current owner. Retracing those steps could be difficult and even impossible, but Pixie was not giving up. She finally had something that resembled evidence, and she was focusing all her energy on it.

Chapter 15
Lost Hope

Behind the scenes, Yolanda and Pixie worked diligently on my case, but it had been months since I had any new information. I was losing hope. I continued to live my life in prison like I had been doing for over five years.

Angel gave birth to my first grandchild, a boy, a few years back, and a couple of years later, my son had a little girl. It broke my heart to think that I would not be able to see them grow up. My children lived their lives, got married, had children, and did all the things I hoped for them, but I still longed for those young faces and tender hearts I left behind. I realized that I would spend the rest of my sentence in prison. Finding Bryan's killer became hopeless, so I continued with life as the prison pie maker and did my best to make a difference with the women I encountered.

I continued my daily work making pies in the prison kitchen, teaching others along the way. Tori began to blossom and was learning to forgive herself for taking her son's life. She was attending counseling and receiving treatment for her mental illness. She, too, was learning to make the best of her life in such a dreadful place. She pledged her life to Jesus Christ and was baptized by Pastor Mel in our makeshift church. The four of us were leading the other women in finding hope and peace, but deep down, I was losing mine.

My relationship with Jacob was fizzling out, too. His letters became less and less, and his visits were sporadic. I wasn't sure if he was struggling with his issues or if he, too, had lost hope of me ever getting out. I was in desperate need of physical touch, a man's touch. A compassionate and comforting touch that I could only get from a man. Unfortunately, when I did see Jacob, we were not allowed to embrace one another because we were not married. I needed so much to feel the warmth of a man. Depression was setting in.

"Jacob, I have been wondering about you. I didn't think you would ever come to visit me again."

"I am sorry, Rach. I have been super busy with work. I started attending AA meetings again, trying to walk a straight line. How are you?"

"I have been thinking a lot about us."

"I think about us too." Jacob touched my hand.

"No, I think we should end whatever this is between us."

"Our friendship? Why would you say such a thing?"

"I am afraid that I am never getting out, and I don't want to give you false hope that someday we may be together."

"I contacted you, knowing you were sentenced to twenty years. There is no false hope, Rachel."

"I want you to be happy. Find someone to love you and be good to you. You deserve that, and I feel as if our relationship is holding you back from it."

"I am not looking to be with anyone. I am trying to focus on getting myself right, and if you get out and we are together, then I will be happy with that too."

"I don't know."

"What is really going on, Rachel?"

"I guess I am sad. I miss my children, and my heart aches to see them and my grandchildren."

"That is understandable, but you still have a chance of getting out of here. Don't lose hope."

"I haven't heard from Yolanda in months. I have no idea what is going on with my case. Maybe she has given up too."

"I heard they recovered a gun from Rainbow Lake."

"When did you hear that? I knew nothing about that."

"I guess it was all over town. I thought you knew."

"No, I didn't know anything about it. Do they know if it is linked to Bryan's murder?"

"I think they are running tests on it, but Rachel, you know that there could be no link. That is probably why Yolanda hasn't told you."

"You are right. It could be nothing. It's these highs and lows that I am struggling with. One minute I am hopeful, and the next minute all that is taken from me."

"Stay strong. They are going to figure this out

sooner than later. Some day you will know everything, and it will all make sense to you."

"Maybe you are right. I have to go. Please send me some encouraging notes."

"I will do what I can. I will visit soon."

"Bye, Jacob."

Jacob and I parted ways. I was feeling low and didn't feel like having lunch. All I wanted to do was bury my head in a pillow and cry, scream and then cry some more. Jo never let me sit there for very long. She made sure I didn't sink too far into a depression. She made jokes or forced me to socialize with the other women. I wasn't feeling it today, though, so I buried my head and slept the rest of the day away.

Chapter 16
You Get One Day

I was very envious of Jo's upbringing. She told me countless stories about how her parents supported her and her sister in their sports, school, and anything they were interested in. She spoke about the lessons that she learned sitting at the kitchen table with her parents. She told me how her father was a prankster and played jokes on all of them. She said they were Christians with strong morals and values. I laid in my bed listening to her talk for hours about her parents and her childhood.

Each time she spoke about them, I could almost imagine myself in her life how things might have been different for me. When she talked about laughing and talking about their days at the kitchen table, I recalled my father falling from his chair too drunk to hold a conversation. I hated my father so much, but she adored hers. Our lives were so different, and I wondered if her parents ever imagined that their daughter would wind up in such a place. Or if they knew that someday she would be teaching women older than her the lessons they taught.

Every time I would get the blues and start feeling sorry for myself, Jo would remind me of what her mother always told her.

"Josy, it is okay to be sad, hurt, and to cry, but don't you stay there. You get one day. After the day is over, you get up, and you keep going. Life still keeps moving even when you don't want it to."

I think it was Jo's mother's way of teaching her strength without taking away from her softness. Jo reminded me on numerous occasions that "you get one day." It was always in the back of my mind. I could have one day to hurt or feel whatever I was feeling, but after that day, I needed to keep going. There was work to do, and people relied on me; life kept moving.

Life did keep moving, whether I was a part of it or not. We can choose to either bury ourselves away from the world or embrace it. In order to embrace all that life has to offer, we must expect the good and bad days. They will come, but they will also pass.

"Rachel, it is time to get up. You have had your day, and those pies aren't going to make themselves."

"Jo, I don't want to get up. I don't know that I even want to live anymore."

"Now you are just talking nonsense. You will get out soon. Be patient, but don't sit here and wallow in self-pity. That is no good for you or anyone. Now get up. You have promised me and all of these women pies. Don't make me drag you to that kitchen."

"Damn it, Jo. Why do you have to be this way?"

"What kind of friend would I be if I just let you lay there feeling sorry for yourself? We all hate this place from time to time, but this is our life for now. Get up and make the most of it. You have good to do."

"Okay, I am getting up."

"You better not be here when I get back."

"Hey, Jo. Thank you for being such a great friend."

"Don't go getting all in your feelings. I want my pies, as you promised."

"Love you, too, Jo." Mocking her resistance to my affection.

I don't know where Jo found her strength. She could have been angry for the hand she was dealt, but instead, she embraced it and was spreading kindness and hope to so many people. I never once heard her complain about her life in prison. I never heard her cuss God for taking her parents or Martin for letting her take the fall. She got up every morning prepared to do good with the work she was doing for others. She could have been a successful lawyer with a lovely home, a family, and a good life outside of here. But not once did I hear her complain. I needed to feed off her positivity and do my good, which was making pies.

I was late arriving to the kitchen. Tori took her

place and stood in for me during my absence. She was doing so well with her responsibilities. I was proud of her, and I imagined it would be the same pride I would have for Angel, watching her grow and develop into a young woman. My children could never be replaced, but in here, Tori became my daughter of sorts. She helped fill a void in my heart that I had. The yearning I felt for my children was filled with pride I felt knowing Tori was making her way through all her pain. I could only hope that my children were finding their way on the outside without me, and I hoped they, too, were able to find someone to fill the void.

Chapter 17
The Code

In every prison, there is an unspoken code. It is a code that tells you where you are placed, who you can associate with, and which side you will be on if things go wrong. Perryville was no different when it came to codes, but everyone intermingled and helped one another for the most part. We were not segregated like a lot of prisons. Our prison didn't have gangs like the gangs on the outside. In here, gangs were formed by race and not affiliations to the gangs out there, but they laid low in here because the other women quickly stopped it. Most of the time, gang members were singled out. They didn't have the backing from their members like they would outside of here, so they had to play by different rules. Our rules.

I didn't understand the race affiliations. I did not believe in racism. I was friends with all people, and I struggled with how those bonds were formed based on their skin color. All the years in the military exposed me to all people, and I never felt a pull towards my race or any other race for that matter. I saw us as people, some I liked and some I didn't, but race never played a part in that.

Everyone was aware of the code, yet we all lived amongst one another and stayed with our group. My group was Jo, who was half Mexican American, Pastor Mel, who was African American, and Tori and I was white. We didn't see color. They were my closest friends, and we loved each other. I hoped that I would never have to choose between my friends and a race because I didn't know what side I would be on. I would be torn, and if it came down to it, I would protect my friends with everything I had in me. I would not pick a side because of race.

"What is going on, Jo?"
"See those two over there?"
"The two Latino girls?"
"Yes. They are from the gang I was in with Martin. I have been watching them for a couple of days. If they figure out who I am, they will probably insist that I join up with them. I think they are trying to put a gang together in here to take over."
"What will that mean?"
"They will try to start recruiting by race. They will start putting pressure on anyone who has a Mexican, Latino background. They will do it mainly by appearance, assuming someone's skin color reveals their heritage. Or if someone speaks Spanish. They have been plotting now for a few days. It looks like they have influence from someone on the outside. I am just hoping they don't recognize me."
"We need to stop this before it starts."
"I am not sure how to do that. That is why I have been watching them plot. I am trying to see what they are up to, but without getting close to them I

will have no way of knowing. I am afraid that Martin has something to do with this. He may have instructed them to find me to head up the gang."

"You can't do that, Jo."

"I know I can't. I don't want to be any part of it."

"What if you refuse?"

"They will put a hit on me to take me out."

"We can't let this happen. What can I do?"

"Right now, I am not sure, but you need to watch your back. Don't shower alone anymore. If you rest during the day, sleep with one eye open. Since you are on the bottom bunk, they will come for you first."

"I guess I now know why you pick the top bunk."

"That is exactly why. If someone comes into our cell, I have time to jump down and put a beating on them before it gets out of hand. We need to just be aware."

"Should we talk to Mel and Tori?"

"I am not too worried about them because they are not my cellmate. Mel can take care of herself, and her being a Pastor will detour any attempts to attack her. Tori needs to lay low and not be with us too much in the open. They are watching everyone. I will talk to some of the women I have helped and see if I can get any information. I have a few that I am in the middle of their cases. They won't turn on me at this point. It is too risky for them. Just be cautious, Rachel. They are up to something."

Jo was well aware of gang life. She tried to steer clear of it, but Martin was able to pull her in. She was not a violent person; she was smart, and using her intelligence was what she needed to do.

If gangs began to form, it would be constant chaos. Of course, we had disagreements and the occasional fistfight, but there weren't stabbings in Perryville. Gangs would bring the violence to a different level. We needed to stop it before it started. Our unit was full of Christian women and women trying to do their time the best they could. Most of them didn't want confrontation either, so fighting against an uprising of a gang would be difficult.

"Tori, meet me in the freezer." I said frantic.

"Okay, what is going on?"

"Just go."

"Rachel, what is going on?"

"Jo has discovered that some gang members are trying to form a Latino gang. She said they are from her L.A. gang and may try to recruit her or expect her to join. You need to steer clear of the both of us until she gets this figured out."

"What about the kitchen and our pies?"

"Keep working; just don't socialize with us too much in the open. Jo is going to talk to Mel, too."

"Okay. You know I will do whatever you say. Should I be scared?"

"Don't be scared, Tori. We are going to sort this out and get these girls out of here."

"Rachel, I can fight."

"Tori, I don't want you to fight." I chuckled.

"Seriously, I grew up with all boys. I have taken my share of ass whooping's, but I have handed them out too. I am not afraid of any of these women."

"I hope it doesn't come to that, but I will keep it in mind if the time does arrive. I am glad to know that you have our backs."

"Rachel, you saved me. I will do whatever it takes to protect you and our friends."

"You're a good kid, Tori. Just be watchful."

I watched at a distance as Jo was approached by one of the gang girls. Jo leaned on the door frame of our cell when the girl walked up to her. The other girl looked on from a table, observing the conversation.

"I know you. You are Martin's girl." The girl said to Jo.

"I am no one's girl." Jo looked in the distance, not making eye contact.

"Oh yes, you are. Martin still claims you. That means you are still his girl. I remember seeing you with him on the outside."

"I have been here for a long time. I don't have any affiliation with Martin any longer. I took the fall for him. I think I proved my loyalty."

"I hear you are the prison lawyer now. If you are so good, why don't you get yourself out."

"You are a fool." Jo snickered and rolled her eyes.

"I am no fool. Martin sends a message."

"I don't care what Martin or you, for that matter, has to say."

"Join us, and we will provide you protection."

"I have done just fine without your protection. Whatever scheme you and your little puppet think you can work out. It won't work in here. We won't tolerate your gang bullshit."

"Who is going to stop us? You? Are you going to stop us, Jo? You know there is only one way in and one way out of the gang."

"Do what you think you have to do, but we will fight you, and you will lose."

"I have never lost a fight, and I don't intend on losing this one. Mark my word. You will join up with us, or you will leave in a body bag."

"Your threats don't intimidate me. I am in here for life. You taking me out doesn't scare me. Hell, you might be doing me a favor. Now get back to your little puppet and let her know that we will stand and the two of you will fall. That you can count on."

We were on high alert. Those on the outside influenced this gang. These women pledged their allegiance to their gang, and they would not back down. For most of them, it was the only life they knew, and they would continue to live it in the prison at all costs. Jo was in danger, and we all knew it, yet she continued to show strength and seemed fearless. The rest of us were preparing for the next step. Would we have to fight to protect her, ourselves, or the quiet lives we were living in this prison? We had to get prepared and make a plan.

"What did she say, Jo?"
"I was right. They think they will force me to join up with them in here. I am not afraid of them."
"We need to call a meeting and get ready for a fight."
"There will be no fight, Rachel."
"So, do we go to the Warden?"
"That is the last thing we will do. A snitch is the worst title you can hold. That will get you killed."

Jo held a meeting in our makeshift church after Sunday service. Her words echoed the halls, and it was the first time I ever heard her speak to a group. She was a true leader. No wonder the gang wanted her on their side.

"Ladies, we are under attack. As some of you know, I was a part of an L.A. gang when I got sentenced here. The prisons in L.A. are overflowing, so they send gang members here to serve their time. We need to rise against these gangs and those that are a part of them. I have recently discovered that two women from my gang are now here in Perryville. They are trying to recruit members to serve their purpose. Their intentions are nothing but evil, and they will do nothing but cause chaos and discord amongst us.

I am not asking you to commit a crime, but I am asking that you steer clear of such affiliations and always protect yourself. We are a mighty force, women of God, and our strength in numbers will push them out. We must stand up against this invasion. Pastor Mel, please lead us in prayer."

The women's faces were overshadowed with fear. Most of them were not violent, nor did they know how to be. Perryville was a comfortable prison to do time in. Just like me, some of these women were living better in prison than they were on the outside. They were not equipped to fight against a gang; they were scared.

"Nice little speech, Jo. Half of that group has already pledged to me. Your time was wasted." The gang girl sat next to Jo during lunch.

"Go sit somewhere else. I don't want to be seen with you. I will tell you again for the last time. You will not win. Now leave."

"Martin said you were stubborn. I like a challenge. Enjoy your lunch."

Chapter 18
The Justice System

From the moment I arrived at Perryville, I felt like I was at home. Now with the fear of gangs and them coming after Jo, I wanted out more than ever. I fought enough through my life, and I didn't think I had the strength to continue to fight. For the most part, I was happy in prison. I was doing okay, and I had a purpose, but I still wanted out.

"Rachel, you have mail."

"Thanks, Jo. Did you get anything from your sister today?"

"No. I haven't heard from her for a while. I am sure she is busy with her husband and children. It's all good. Who is your letter from?"

"The Innocence Project." I opened the letter as tears flowed down my face. I was devastated.

"What does it say?"

"The court denied my appeal. I guess you are stuck with me."

Jo wrapped her arms around me as I sobbed. She was not affectionate, but she knew that this letter meant I would never get to see my grandchildren grow up. She knew how hard Yolanda, Pixie, and even she had fought for me. It was a battle we all lost, but I felt the most defeated. It was over for me.

I never understood the justice system. You get locked up but are supposedly innocent until proven guilty. That is not how it works. You are guilty until you can prove you are innocent. If you don't have the financial means to fight a case, you will likely serve time.

How many people are innocent, sitting in prison because of someone's ego? How many of them have been wrongly accused due to mistaken identity or were in the wrong place at the wrong time? How many women are away from their children because the only way they could get away from an abusive situation was to kill their abuser? Where is the justice for those people? Who is fighting for those people?

Those judges who denied my appeal do not know me as a person. They sit on their high horse and throw down judgment without remorse. Everyone has a story, but no one is listening. They are discarding us like animals instead of finding a way to help us live a better life. Without guidance, without love, anyone could end up in here. What the hell is wrong with our justice system?

"Rachel, your lawyer is here to see you."
"Oh, now she wants to show up," I said sarcastically.
"Hello, Rachel. I am sorry you received your letter before I was able to visit."
"Yeah, kind of a blow."

"I am still fighting for you. We recovered a gun from Rainbow Lake. We have traced the original owner, but that owner has no connection and lives in Ohio."

"I heard about the gun. So now what?"

"How did you hear about it?"

"My friend Jacob. He used to live on the mountain. He now lives in Phoenix and visits from time to time. He said everyone on the mountain was talking about it."

"I didn't think it was common knowledge. I will be sure to talk with Pixie about it."

"I don't know; maybe he knows someone on the police force. He didn't say."

"The original owner sold it years ago. He is trying to round up a copy of the receipt. It could lead to the killer."

"Does it match the weapon used to kill Bryan?"

"It does, but to have your conviction overturned, we have to find the killer. That is the only way now. We have to prove someone else killed Bryan to prove you didn't."

"This is so messed up. What if you never find his killer. That means I will spend twenty years in prison for a crime I didn't commit. I can't be the only one going through this. This is not justice."

"Rachel, I know you are angry. I don't blame you. I would say, had you not confessed, you might not be here, but I am not sure I believe that either. They already believed you killed him. You were the only person that had a motive."

"Apparently not because I didn't kill him. What about Mr. Andrews? I thought you were going to force him to help us?"

"Now that he is a judge, I can't get anything out of him. I should have buried him when I had the chance. Now he is using his authority to push back and keep me at a distance. I knew he was a lying sack of shit and fed me some sad story about his mother to fend me off."

"So, there is nothing else. Wait to see if the killer shows up."

"I am sorry, Rachel. I have exhausted all of my resources. We have nothing at the moment."

"You tried. I guess I better figure out how to fight."
"What?"

"Gangs are trying to take over in here. If I am going to be in here for the next fifteen years, I guess I better be prepared."

"Rachel, you can't commit a crime. If you do, it could cost you your release."

"Does it really matter at this point, Yolanda? I am not getting out. Let's face it."

"I will still do everything I can do. I will be in touch, Rachel."

At every turn, I had to shift gears. I couldn't think about my release now. Finding Bryan's killer was the only way I was getting out. The police didn't even have fingerprints or DNA to compare to. The only way his killer would be revealed is if they confessed. Who was going to do that if they knew they got away with it?

My focus was now on the fight at hand. We needed to stop the gang from forming. We needed to push them out and regain our peace. I knew I wouldn't make it if I had to fight daily. I was getting older, and I was wearing down. We needed to do something soon.

Chapter 19
The Fight

A fight to save our peace was inevitable. We were going to have to do something; we had no other choice. There was an eerie calmness that came over our unit. Everyone knew something was coming, but when. It reminded me of the same calm that always fell right before Bryan, and I had a huge blow-up. I used to brace myself for what was to come. Now I was in fight mode, just like I had always been for years living with an abusive husband. I could do this; I spent years fighting a man. Fighting these women would be a walk in the park, or so I thought. I believed we would fight with our fists—old school, like fighting on the playground after school. I was not prepared for the ruthlessness that came along with being in a gang. These women didn't fight fair, and neither would we.

I couldn't believe that this is what my life had come to. It was like we were fighting for land or territory. I didn't want to have enemies. I wanted to live peacefully amongst everyone, but I chose my side. I would stand alongside Jo, Mel, and Tori. We would fight for what we worked so hard to accomplish, which was unity, love, and peace. Not everyone wants unity. Some see divide among race as strength, but the four of us saw it as a weakness.

Together, our different races and backgrounds had built a solid foundation, and we would not let anyone take it from us. It was time to fight.

"Once everyone is seated for chow, you and I will make our way to the Latinos."
"Got it!" I responded.
"Mel, you and Tori will be on the lookout. If anyone jumps in, quickly stop them. This could turn ugly quickly. I don't know who they have been able to recruit, so we could get overpowered. Defeating them in a fight makes them lose credibility. We must win."

We treated the day like a normal day. We gathered our trays and sat down at our usual table. It was quiet. Rumors had spread of a fight, but we were unsure of where they were coming from. Everyone was on high alert anticipating something happening any day. I don't know if the guards were aware or if they noticed the quietness that fell on the room. Surely, they knew something was aloof. They were outnumbered, and a lot could happen before they would be able to stop it.
Jo looked around as we ate our meal. She looked at me and then nodded. It was time. I got up from my chair and walked over to the trays like I was putting my tray up. Jo was a few steps behind me.

I quickly moved to the Latinos and swung my tray, hitting one of them upside her head. Jo came from the other direction and hit the other girl the same.

Women began to swiftly move their chairs away from the table and back against the walls. Most of them were onlookers. Jo and I fought the women for several minutes, rolling on the floor and then back on our feet. The noise was overpowering. Women were yelling and cheering, mostly for us but others for their gang. We needed to win this fight, and as we continued, in the distance, Bell was taking note of who was rooting for the gang members. They would soon be our target, and we would force them to denounce their affiliation to stay out of harm's way.

We were winning. Blood was everywhere from the blows the Latinos had taken from us. We took a few hits, but we proved our power when the guards charged in with full face masks and riot gear. Quickly, everyone laid on their bellies with their arms behind their backs. It was over.

Jo and I were swiftly taken to solitary. We knew solitary would be our punishment and planned for our time away from our duties as the prison lawyer and the prison pie maker. A fight always constitutes solitary confinement; we weren't surprised by the actions of the guards.

I enjoyed my short time in solitary. It was lonely, but the quietness helped me reflect and regain my peace. I used my time alone to pray and get right with God. I didn't want to become a ruthless person, but you have to do many things to survive in a place like a prison.

Upon the release of our stint in solitary, Jo and I returned to find that we had been separated. She would no longer be my cellmate. Neither of us expected that outcome. We had been living together for over five years. It was heartbreaking.

Jo was assigned a cell with no roommate. She didn't mind the alone time as she read and worked most days. I was roomed with a young Indian girl. I kept my distance from her. I was more cautious now, and with the uprising, I didn't know who I could trust.

I visited with Jo every day, even though I was not allowed in her cell. I missed our nightly conversations that helped me go to sleep. I felt lost without her.

"How do things look? Did we accomplish what we needed to?" I asked Jo.

"Other than most of the women fearing you and me, I am not sure what we accomplished."

"Have you had any interaction with the Latinos since we got out of solitary?"

"No, and I heard that the one is supposed to be released soon. It makes me think she turned on someone to be getting out so early. If she did, she wouldn't make it long on the outside. She will have to do something to lengthen her stay. So, watch your back."

"I will stay aware. I miss you, Jo. I am not sure I would have agreed to all this if I knew we would be separated."

"Yeah, I didn't expect that. I miss you too."

The Latino gang members became quiet and stagnant. They lost their credibility by losing a fight to Jo and me. Most people knew that Jo and I were in prison for murder, but few knew that we hadn't committed the crimes. Those charges gave us credit as ruthless criminals; one's that were capable of killing someone. We had control over our unit again, but we were ruling by fear instead of grace this time. The invasion of gang members forced us to become people we didn't want to become. It started to look like a real prison, one with hardened criminals instead of women wanting to change their lives. Few gang members changed in prison. They were ruled by their leaders no matter where they went, and prison gave them the ability to continue their crimes, only closer to their enemies. Gang members who do time earn a great deal of respect on the outside. They would not pass up the opportunity to pursue their goals and rise in the ranks.

"Rachel, come quick. Jo is hurt."

"What? Where?" I threw my apron down and ran as fast as I could behind Tori.

"Where is she? What happened? Where the fuck is she?" I shouted as all the women stood around staring.

When I got to Jo's cell, she was already gone. The EMTs had taken her away. Her cell floor was covered in blood. It looked like she was in her bunk when she was attacked. Her sheets were soiled, and her books were thrown about. She put up a fight, but she was ambushed.

"Tell me right now who did this," I shouted to the women looking on with shock.

"I will kill whoever is behind this. Where are the Latinos? Bring them to me, now. I know they did this."

"Rachel, they are gone. The guards took them." Tori put her arm around me.

I banged on the two-way glass at the guards.

"Tell me what is going on. Jo is my friend."

"Come on, Rachel, let's go pray for Jo." Pastor Mel and Tori led me to our church as I cried out for my friend.

"I will get justice for Jo," I screamed all through the halls.

I was filled with so much anger as Pastor Mel began praying for Jo's healing. I couldn't pray; all I could do was think about revenge. Jo didn't deserve this; she was a kind soul, and I would revenge this senseless act.

"Pastor Mel, a guard is asking for you."

"I am on my way. Tori, stay here with Rachel and pray."

"You are the prison Pastor?" The guard asked.

"Yes."

"I am to inform you that Jo was stabbed eight times. She is in surgery and should have a full recovery."

"Thank you. Who told you to come to me?"

"The Warden."

"Praise Jesus." Pastor Mel raised her hand in praise. She swiftly returned to Tori and me as other women joined us in prayer.

"What did they say?"

"Jo was stabbed eight times. She is in surgery, but they expect a full recovery. Praise Jesus, ladies. Our Lord is a healer. Continue to pray."

"I will get whoever did this," I said.

"You will do no such thing, Rachel. "Vengeance is mine says the Lord."

"Aren't you angry, Mel?"

"We cannot fall to anger. In anger, we do foolish things. Control your anger and know that God will make this right. He will not forsake her; she is His child."

"I don't understand you people. Our friend could

die, and no one is doing anything. God is not doing anything."

"Rachel, I love you, but you will not curse God in my presence or my church. You need to pray, or you need to leave."

"I will leave."

I could not control the anger I had for what was done to Jo. I could not imagine my life in prison without her by my side. She was the reason I was doing everything I was doing. She was the closest thing I had to a sister; she was family. I wanted everyone else to share in my anger, and I wanted revenge. I left Mel and Tori and retreated to my cell. I paced in my cell, contemplating my plan to get justice for Jo.

What would I do without Jo in my life?

Chapter 20
The New Warden

Warden Johnson never experienced bloodshed while he was Warden at Perryville. He took Jo's attack as a sign that he could no longer do good in a place that was being overrun by evil. He soon resigned.

Our new Warden was a haggard old woman from New York. Her name was Warden Shay, and she would soon put an end to all the good that Warden Johnson had implemented. She believed none of us were worthy of rehabilitation, activities that furthered our education or bettered us for our futures. She thought prison should be a scary place, ensuring crimes would not be committed in fear of being locked up.

Warden Johnson believed the opposite of Warden Shay. He worked for years to bring skill development programs, education programs, and he was the reason Jo was able to be the prison lawyer, and I was the prison pie maker. His resignation would soon affect us all, and Perryville would become one of Arizona's roughest prisons.

As Jo recovered in a local hospital, the rest of us prepared for the changes that would take place with the new Warden. We were uncertain of our futures, and we were unsure if we could maintain the peace that we worked so hard to establish. The women were growing restless.

Warden Shay put the entire prison on lockdown for 24-hours to show her authority. We had regained peace after the Latino gang members were put in solitary, and Jo was taken to the hospital. It was quiet, so there was no reason for her lockdown other than she wanted us to know there was a new Warden in town.

Tori and I were locked out of the kitchen during the 24-hour lockdown. We needed to get access as soon as possible if we were going to make our monthly pie quota. We were both getting anxious, but we had no way of communicating with one another.

My new cellmate and I rarely spoke. When we did, it was more out of being courteous than anything. We had nothing in common. She was young, arrogant, and defiant in every way, like a spoiled child. She worked harder at finding a way around the rules instead of abiding by them, and I was growing impatient with her. I missed Jo so much. I am not sure I could ever replace her as a friend, cellmate, or mentor.

Tori and I rushed to the kitchen as soon as the lockdown was released. In the doorway stood the Warden and Bell, the kitchen super.

"Ladies, your pie-making days are over. Take your personal belongings and don't come back to the kitchen unless you plan to peel potatoes or wash dishes." The Warden said in her New York accent.

"Why would you do this? We have a good thing going here. Women are learning a skill, and we are providing something special for the other women to look forward to." I plead.
"Prison isn't for learning and special days. Gather your things and go."

Bell's eyes filled with tears as she watched our hearts break. There was nothing she could do but stand by the Warden and ensure we gathered our things; she was heartbroken too. I will never forget the first day she tried my pie. A friendship was formed from that day on, and Bell was the reason I was able to make pies and teach others. She knew the kitchen brought joy to many of the women working in it. She also knew the kitchen, and making pies saved Tori. What would become of all of us without it?
Tori and I hung our heads as we walked back to our cells. The other women stared, unsure why we weren't in the kitchen where we were every day for the last few years. It was a sad day for everyone.
I stood up in the common area to make the announcement.

"Ladies, Warden Shay has shut down our pie-making. I am sorry to inform you that we will no longer have a pie day once a month. I do not know her reason behind this, but we are no longer allowed in the kitchen."

All the women began booing and throwing chairs all over the room. I didn't stop them; I was angry, too. Quickly a guard came out of nowhere and threw me to the ground.

"What did I do? I didn't do anything."
"You are encouraging defiance and rioting."
"All I did was tell them that we will no longer have pies."
"The Warden wants you to put in solitary until you can learn to keep your mouth shut."
"I didn't fucking do anything."

I spent two weeks in solitary. That was longer than the stint Jo and I spent for the fight with the Latinos. Warden Shay was not messing around, and she was using all means possible to force her hand.
I was happy to see Jo when I turned the corner headed towards my cell after my release. My face lit up, and so did hers when our eyes met. She was fifty or sixty pounds lighter. She looked good and healthy. We both needed each other; we embraced.

"How are you feeling?"
"Pretty good. I am still a little sore in the gut, but that will pass."

"You look good, Jo."

"Thanks. Maybe I needed to be stabbed to lose a few pounds." We both laughed. "I hear the Warden shut down the pie-making."

"Yeah, and then sent me to solitary for telling everyone. She is a soulless bitch."

"I am probably next. I don't know if she knows about my closet. I am trying to be as discreet as possible. I need to do what I have been doing. Most of these women can't afford lawyers. I am the closest thing they have."

"What will we do without your services? Will, she shut Pastor Mel down next?"

"I don't know, but without some hope, these women will turn on each other, and it will be complete chaos in here."

"What can we do?"

"We can't do anything. Welcome to prison, where someone else decides your fate. We didn't know how good we had it with Warden Johnson."

"This sucks. What am I going to do now without the kitchen? What is Tori going to do?"

"We just keep going. Maybe you can get involved with the ministry. Surely the Warden won't shut that down. She would have to be completely heartless not to allow the church."

"I think Mel is mad at me. I cursed God in the church the day you got stabbed."

"I am sure she has forgiven you. Forgiveness is kind of her thing."

Chapter 21
Forgiveness

We all tried to continue doing some good, even though the Warden shut down everything that gave us hope. I was struggling to find my place in our new situation. I didn't know how to do anything other than making pies. My days that used to be filled with teaching and creating were exchanged with boredom and hopelessness. I wanted out.

"Rachel, I don't feel so good. Go get a guard."
"Jo, what is wrong? You are white as a ghost."
"Go, Rachel, something is really wrong."
"Help, someone, help us," I yelled.

The guards rushed to Jo, and she was soon taken on a gurney out of the prison. None of us knew what was wrong with her, but she was sick. She held her stomach, and her face lost all color as they carried her off. We could only suspect that her injuries were causing her difficulty.

Again, I couldn't do anything to help her. I couldn't be with her for comfort. She was fighting for her life, alone in a hospital somewhere in Arizona. I needed to pray; I needed to do something. I went to our church and knelt, folding my hands on a metal chair. I couldn't pray. All I could think was how angry God must be at me for my actions. I was not a child of God; I didn't act like a child of God. This place had turned me into a person I never wanted to be. I hated it even more now than ever.

"Hey, Rachel. I am glad to see you back here."
"Mel, I am so sorry for my actions before. I love Jo, and I can't stand to see her going through this. I am so filled with anger towards those women for doing this to her. How do I get past that? How do I find forgiveness in my heart for those who have done us wrong?"
"One of the hardest things to do is forgive. I struggled for a long time with the same issue. What I have learned through the years is the hardest person to forgive is ourselves. It would help if you started there. Rachel, you need to forgive yourself because sometimes the anger that we hold has nothing to do with others but with us. Ask God to help you forgive yourself for the wrong you have done, and then you will begin to have a heart of forgiveness."
"I don't hurt people, though. What am I supposed to forgive?"
"I can't tell you what things go through your mind. I can't tell you the things that keep you up at night. You are the only one who knows what you have done or haven't done. You need to let some things go. God will help you. Just call out to him."

Mel left me alone as I contemplated what things I needed to forgive myself for. She was right. Admitting to ourselves that we have failed, that we, too, hurt others is hard, but I needed to dig deep and let go.

"God, I don't know what I am doing. I want to forgive, and I don't want to have all this anger that I have. Help me get past it."

A calmness fell over me as I sobbed and prayed. I needed to forgive myself for a lot of reasons. For so long, I held such guilt for letting men in my life hurt me. I blamed myself for not being strong enough to stand up to my father. For not being strong enough to leave a man who hurt me physically and mentally, and most importantly, that I wasn't strong enough to protect my children. That I allowed them to suffer because I selfishly wanted to be loved so bad that I couldn't recognize the pain they must have endured. Those were the things that kept me awake at night. I needed to release it. It wasn't anger that I had for others; it was the anger I had towards myself. I needed to learn to forgive myself too.

I stayed in our church for several hours. Mel returned a short time later to find me still in the kneeling position. She knelt beside me and put her arm around me.

"I can pray with you if you would like."

"Just sit here with me, please."

"I can do that, too. Rachel, you will make it through this, but you won't make it alone. I am here for you always, even if I just need to sit here quietly with you."

"Thank you."

I don't know how long we sat there in silence, but I knew that she was praying even though Mel wasn't saying anything out loud. I knew she had been where I was sitting, and I knew she felt all those things, too. If anyone understood, she did. Maybe if I began to forgive myself, then others, soon I could find some hope again.

Jo never made it back to Perryville. She remained in the hospital for months suffering from an infection. Sadly, when you are a prisoner serving a life sentence, your health is not the utmost concern. Jo was given less than fair medical treatment, and she was not allowed pain medications to help ease her suffering. Once again, the system failed her.

When Jo didn't return after a few months, the Warden was told about her makeshift office, and soon she began removing all of the books and files. Word of the clean out spread through the prison. Many of us showed up to the library and watched as the guards carried out everything Jo had fought so hard to build. We were all devastated. Not just for Jo, but for every woman who needed her knowledge and assistance. It was a massive loss for us all.

We quietly held hands as we looked on. I somewhat felt sorry for the guards. There were some good people amongst them, and you could see the sadness on their faces. Jo touched many lives, including some of those guards. This was no longer about prison and the crimes that had been committed. This was about people, love, and the selfless acts that we all watched Jo do. She cared about the women in that prison, and she spent her time doing good things to help them. None of us could repay her, we couldn't be with her, and we couldn't do anything but look on as they destroyed her life's work.

Chapter 22
The Big Blow

After watching the destruction of Jo's office and everything she so selflessly worked for, I found myself sinking into a depression. Even rethinking her words "You get one day" still didn't help me move past all that was happening. For several years I felt as if I could make it in prison. I had a decent life, and I was making a difference. Now I had no purpose, I didn't have Jo to help me see the brighter side of things, and I felt like everything was crumbling around me.

The only hope for me was my visits with Jacob. The thought of having a life with him someday was the one thing I was holding on to.

"Hi, Rachel. I am glad to see you. It has been a while. I tried to visit but was told you weren't allowed visitors."

"I am glad to see you, too, Jacob."

"You look worn down. What is going on?"

"This place is no longer safe. Jo is in the hospital. Some gang members stabbed her, and now I fear they will come for me.

"Why would they come for you?"

"We fought them, and they lost. Then the gang members attacked Jo while she slept. I don't know if she will make it."

"Oh my God, Rachel."

"Warden Johnson resigned after the incident, and it hasn't been the same since."

"I heard about his resignation on the news, but they didn't say why."

"I know it had something to do with Jo. Things were peaceful in here before that happened."

"Well, you still have your pies."

"No. The new Warden shut it down shortly after we got out of solitary confinement. I can't even go to the kitchen. She cleaned out Jo's office yesterday. Everything is gone."

"Jesus, Rachel. Have you heard anything about your case? Maybe you will get out soon."

"I haven't heard anything for a good while. The only way I am getting out is if Bryan's killer confesses. I am probably going to die in this place."

"Don't think that way, Rachel. Maybe something will come up."

"Enough about my crazy life. How are things for you?"

"I was offered a job in Texas, but I am not going to take it. I wouldn't be able to see you, and now I don't want to leave you."

"Take the job, Jacob. This is my life now. I am not getting out, and you need to move on. You deserve it, and I want you to be happy."

"I know I can't do anything from the outside, but at least I can visit."

"You can't do anything to help my situation. Move

on with your life. I appreciate everything you have done for me and been to me over these years. Take the job."

"Rachel, I don't want to move on without you. I love you, Rachel."

"If only love could get me out of here. Take care of yourself. Go be happy."

"Rachel." Jacob yelled as I got up and walked away.

"Bye, Jacob."

That was the last time I would ever see Jacob. I wanted him to live his life. The hope of us ever being together was gone. He had been a wonderful friend and confidant while serving my time. I felt lucky to have him in my life, but I knew it was time to let him go. I didn't want to hold him back from finding love and finding happiness.

After that visit, I received a few letters, but I didn't respond, and I took Jacob off of my visitor list. Soon, the letters stopped, and I did my best to erase him from my mind. This was my life now. I needed to figure out how to survive. I went from being a wife and mother trying to survive to a prisoner trying to survive. Sometimes the two lives didn't seem much different.

I began spending my days reading in the church. It was the quietest place in the prison so that I could concentrate. It amazed me how much Jo read. I struggled to get through one book, reading chapters repeatedly because I couldn't retain the information.   146

Jo could quote whole books from beginning to end. She was much smarter than I realized.

"Rachel, you have a visitor."
"I am not taking visitors."
"It's your lawyer."

I closed my book and shuffled to the main door. I could only imagine that Yolanda was there to deliver bad news, and I didn't need another blow like the last few I received. I didn't look forward to our meeting.

"If you are here to give me bad news, you can leave. I have endured enough of that."
"Why would you think I have bad news."
"Why else would you be here?"
"I know this is hard. I have heard about some of the things going on. I am sorry, Rachel, that you have to go through this."
"You have no idea," I began to sob. "I can't take it anymore. I am not a criminal. I don't know how to live like a criminal or survive like one."
"We are getting you out, Rachel. We have new evidence. The guy in Ohio that originally owned the gun has located the receipt. We have a name, and we are following up on the lead. This could be Bryan's killer."
"Then what happens next."

"I am trying to stay quiet about it. We need to locate the individual and bring him in for questioning."

"So, it could be nothing?"

"It is something. We are getting closer. I told you this takes time."

"It has been almost six years. How much more time do I have to stay in this God-awful place?"

"Just hold on."

"I don't know if I can take much more, Yolanda."

"I know. I am doing everything I can. I know you are innocent, and soon so will everyone else."

"Thank you."

"I will let you know as soon as I know something. Hang in there."

I wanted to be hopeful, but every time I was, something else stopped me. I needed to no longer think about getting out and just focus on getting through my sentence.

Chapter 23
The Plan

Behind the scenes, Yolanda and my children were planning for my release. Yolanda was confident that she would soon uncover Bryan's murderer, and I would be set free. I had been locked up for almost six years. My children would need to help me financially get on my feet and to reinsert my life back into society. Yolanda knew she would need their help. She refrained from letting me know their plans because she didn't want to give me hope, but she also knew that they needed to prepare their lives to make room for me. We would all have to adjust.

"Thank you both for meeting with me. I know it has been difficult for you all. I believe we are close to finding Bryan's murderer. I have detectives tracking down the person who purchased the gun from Ohio. If we can locate him and trace the gun to him, I believe we can get your mom out."

"How long do you think this will take?" Adam asked.

"The person we are tracing has moved multiple times throughout the years, but if they left a good trail, it could be soon."

"Will they have to have a trial first?"

"It depends. If the person confesses, no. If they

deny their involvement, then yes, a trial would have to take place to convict someone else. It is possible that we can get a release based on the discovery, but that takes time too."

"What do we need to do?"

"First, you need to decide where your mother will be going when she is released. She will need some time to reacquaint herself with the outside. We will need to have transportation ready for her upon her release. Do you know where she is going? I know you two live in different states."

"I don't have room for her," Adam said.

"She is going to come home with me to Indiana. I will make room for her, and we have family there that can help."

"I will secure a flight for her once she is released, but you will need to pay for your travel. Can you do that?"

"I can put some money back for it, yes."

"Do you both plan to be there for her release?"

"Yes, we do." Adam and Angel looked at one another.

"I will find out what size clothes she is wearing these days so we can have something for her to wear. She has probably lost or gained weight since she was arrested. They probably don't have her old clothes anyway."

"Once you find out, I can get her some things. She has nothing at this point. I wasn't able to hang onto any of her things. I have moved a few times too."

150

"I will keep in touch with you both. We need to stay quiet about our discovery. We don't want someone getting word of it and tipping off the person we think did this."

"Do you know who it is?"

"I do, but I will not reveal that until it is time."

"We understand," Angel responded.

"As soon as I am sure, you will be the first to know. Then I am going to burry that son of a bitch, Mr. Andrews, for doing this to your mother."

"We can't thank you enough, Yolanda."

"It has been a pleasure to help Rachel. I am just sorry it has taken this long."

"We hope to hear from you soon. Good-bye."

Yolanda continued to work on my case. She didn't tell me she found Bryan's killer. Yolanda wanted to make sure everything was in place before she revealed the information. Before I could be released, Bryan's killer would need to be arrested, tried, and convicted, but Yolanda hoped she would get a confession before any of that happened.

I didn't know any of the things going on outside of those four walls until I watched the news with Tori.

"Mr. Andrews, is it true you helped convict an innocent woman when you were supposed to help her?"

I sat in shock as I watched television reporters surrounding Mr. Andrews asking him questions about my case.

"Isn't that the guy?" Tori asked.
"Yes. Mr. Andrews was my public defender."
"Rachel, I think they are talking about your case. Are you getting out?"
"Tori, I don't know what is going on."

We continued to watch as the reporters threw one question after another at Mr. Andrews. I was learning about my case by watching the news. I was confused, in shock and hopeful.

"Mr. Andrews, you are now a judge. Will this reflect poorly for you and your position?"
"I have done nothing wrong. Mrs. Havens confessed to the murder of her husband. That is all I will say." Mr. Andrews got into his car as the reporters continued with their questions.
"An innocent woman has been in prison for six years, and you did nothing to help her. Wasn't your job to help people like her?"

We watched Mr. Andrews drive off as the reporter finished.

"Mr. Andrews was the public defender in Mrs. Havens case. Discovery in the case has revealed that Mrs. Havens did not kill her husband but was coerced into a confession by Mr. Andrews. Mrs. Havens has been fighting her case since her incarceration six years ago. It has been revealed that The Innocence Project took on her case because they believed she was wrongly convicted. Mrs. Havens has been serving her sentence in an Arizona prison but could soon be released with this discovery. We will keep you up to date as we learn more about this injustice. Back to you, Bob."

"You are getting out, Rachel." Tori grabbed me and hugged me.

"I won't believe it until I am walking out that door."

"You are going to be famous."

"Famous." I laughed.

"You are going to be on television. They have to do something now."

"I just want out, and I want whoever killed Bryan to pay for the crime. But I am enjoying watching Mr. Andrews take some heat for what he did."

"Yeah, that bastard needs to pay."

"I wish Jo was here for this."

"Me too, Rachel. Me, too."

Chapter 24
Closing In

"Yolanda, what the hell is going on? I can't even get into my house without reporters all over me."

"Well, hello, Pete."

"Why are you doing this to me?"

"I told you if you didn't help me get my client out of prison that I would bury you and your career for what you did to her."

"I didn't do anything to her. I wanted to help her, but she confessed."

"Come on, Pete, we have been over this. I gave you ample opportunities to help me. You refused, so now I am letting everyone know what kind of a public defender, judge, and man you are. You did this to yourself."

"Don't do this, Yolanda. How are you getting her out anyway?"

"We found Bryan's killer; no thanks to you."

"Has the killer been prosecuted? How do you know that you found the right person? Aren't you jumping the gun here?"

"It's him. We have linked him back to Bryan and his motive to kill him. He purchased a gun in Ohio years ago, planning this for a long time. We have him backed into a corner. There is no way out for him at this point. I am sure he will confess to a lesser sentence. He is the killer."

"Then why ruin me. If Mrs. Havens is getting out, then why do you need to do this to me?"

"Pete, you took an oath to help people. You didn't help Rachel when you could have. I even gave you a chance to redeem yourself, but you refused. You deserve whatever becomes of this."

"I will be ruined. My career, my reputation, and possibly my family."

"I took an oath, too, Pete. The difference between you and me is that I took my oath seriously, and that was to right the wrongs that have been done to innocent people. I have pledged my life to fight the injustices in this country. Those injustices usually happen because people like you care more about a career than a human being. Mrs. Havens has suffered a great deal because of you, and I will not let that go unpunished."

"Yolanda, I am begging you don't do this."

"It is done. I have contacted every newspaper and television station from Indiana to Arizona. You are finished. Look at the bright side. At least you won't be going to prison. You will still have your freedom, unlike Mrs. Havens. Count yourself fortunate."

Yolanda accomplished what she set out to do, and that was to ruin Mr. Andrews. He soon resigned from his position as judge and shortly after moved out of Indiana to avoid the backlash from my case. He had the chance to make things right, but he decided to let me suffer in prison while he lived his comfortable life. It wasn't fair, and although he wasn't the only one who played a role in my conviction, he was the main character.

The detectives were closing in on Bryan's killer and were led right to Arizona. Pixie was right. It was someone who knew us and knew us well. A gun purchased in Ohio 2,000 miles from Arizona was the murder weapon. Whoever killed Bryan must have tracked him down. But who and why?

"Yolanda, it's Pixie. I have a swat team ready to go in for the arrest. It is happening today."

"Please keep me updated. I am booking a flight now. I want to see why he wanted Bryan dead. None of this has made sense."

"Have you told Rachel?"

"No. I haven't said anything. I told her children to be prepared for her release, but I didn't want to tell Rachel until we knew we could get her out. It has been rough for her, and I didn't want to give her false hope. I can't wait until I get to see her walk out of that place."

Yolanda hopped on the next flight to Arizona. By the time she arrived, a swat team would have already apprehended the suspect. She planned for a long night listening to the interrogation. She would be able to observe, but nothing else. Her role was to defend me, not prosecute the killer. It would be hard for her not to be able to say anything or ask

156

questions. She wanted to know why just as much as everyone else.

"Pixie, did you make the arrest? I just landed. I can come now."
"No need, Yolanda."
"Why? What happened? Did you not make the arrest?"
"Our swat team went in, but he was expired when they arrived."
"Expired? Layman's terms, Pixie."
"The suspect was dead, and it appeared as if he had been for a couple of weeks."
"Dead? You have got to be kidding me. No fucking way this is happening."
"It is over, Yolanda. Meet me for dinner. I have something for you."

Yolanda sat in her rental car at the airport and cried as she pounded her fist against the steering wheel. She put everything she had into fighting for me. If this person was Bryan's killer, I would not be getting out. She needed an arrest, a confession, and a conviction. Pixie and Yolanda met at a café close to the airport. Yolanda would be flying back to New York sooner than she expected with the events that took place.

"Pixie, have a seat. Tell me what happened."
"Are you okay?"

"I have put everything into this case. What a blow. Just when I thought I was going to get Rachel out, this happens. What now?"

"I think you will be happy to know that Bryan's killer has been found."

"What good is that going to do if he is dead?"

Pixie handed Yolanda an envelope with two letters in it. "You need to read this."

Yolanda opened the letters and read them one by one, looking up at Pixie with shock. The letters revealed everything and answered every question that we all had for so long. I was getting out.

"Now go get Rachel out."

Chapter 25
Pre-release

Yolanda jumped into her rental car and caught the next plan out of Arizona. She arrived at her office in New York late into the night, but that didn't stop her from preparing the forms to present to the judge the next morning. It took several days to get my release in order. She contacted my children and prepared them for what was to come. In a few weeks, maybe months, I could be free, but I knew nothing of it.

Inside I was still fighting my depression. I laid low, not wanting to cause any disturbance resulting in more solitary confinement or privileges taken away. The women coming into Perryville were younger and younger, and I didn't have the strength to mentor them or show them the ropes. I avoided almost everyone. I was exhausted by the drama and the time invested in trying to change lives. After the Warden took everything from us, there was nothing for any of us to look forward to. To help others, you have to spend a lot of your energy helping them buy into the idea of a better life. I didn't have that kind of energy anymore, and there was nothing to have them buy into. We were criminals, animals in the minds of everyone on the outside. We didn't deserve anything but the harshest of treatment, but what most of those people fail to understand is that half of the women locked up are innocent or could be rehabilitated. Most of these women in prison committed crimes because they ran out of choices. They didn't have help, and the people who were supposed to help them didn't. What prison did for these women was turn them into real criminals because to survive in a place like that, you have to commit criminal acts. You must become hardened and ruthless. The young women who walk in here after the system has failed them turn into what none of us want them to become. They become unable to save, they become a product of their environments, and they become just another number in a messed up system.

I began to test my theory, so I took every opportunity to talk to the women about how they got here. I wanted to see how many of them were actually ruthless and heartless criminals and how many of them were truly here because the system failed them. I took lots of notes and compiled those notes into a book of sorts. Maybe someday, I could show how our justice system doesn't help the victim but throws them away, so they don't have to deal with the real issues. Here are some of their stories.

Mary.
Mary was twenty-four years old when she was

given a life sentence for murdering her uncle in Texas. Mary told me that she came from a dysfunctional family and was molested and raped by several of her uncles throughout her adolescence. She said it seemed accepted in her family, but she never understood why. She told me that there was a lot of drug use and alcoholism that played a huge part in the abuse. She said to me that several of her family members were here illegally, and it was a family code that you didn't do anything to jeopardize their freedom. She was expected to protect them regardless of what they did to not be sent back to Mexico.

Mary was smart and beautiful. When she arrived at Perryville, she was noticeably broken and damaged, but you could still see the beauty. You could tell that she had been through horrible things in her life, but she always smiled, and she still helped other women. She was kind and loving despite all that she had been through. So, I asked why she killed her uncle, even though I could understand after she told me she was molested and raped.

Mary told me that she was able to steer clear of the abuse after she was old enough to work and stay away from home. She said she slept with a piece of iron pipe under her pillow, prepared for an attack from one of those uncles. One night, Mary went home after work to her small family home, where eight adults and several children also lived. When she arrived around midnight she heard screaming coming from a small back porch off of the house. She went to investigate and found one of her uncles forcing himself on her seven-year-old cousin. She said when she locked eyes with her cousin, who was screaming for someone to help her, Mary knew she had to do something. So, she ran to her room, retrieved her iron pipe, and beat her uncle to death. The house was raided, and several people were arrested. Mary told me that she shamed her family because of the arrests resulting in several of them being deported not because she killed her uncle. She also told me that she didn't know why she did it other than that she saw the fear on her cousin's face, and she understood that fear. She wanted to do for her cousin what no one had done for her. Protect her.

Shady (I don't think that is her real name). Shady approached me about writing down her story after she heard I was compiling stories from the other women. She said people needed to know what happened to her. I agreed.

Shady's mother was an addict, and Shady was born into a life of addiction. When she was just an infant, her mother sold her to a preacher and his wife in the local grocery store parking lot so she would have money for drugs. The preacher wanted to keep Shady, but they knew the right thing to do was turn her over to child services and fight to adopt her. So that is what they did. For years the preacher and his wife fought to get custody of Shady, exhausting all of their resources, but the court kept giving her mother chance after chance to get a job, get clean and find a place to live. Each time she would, and each time the preacher and his wife had to hand Shady back over to her mother. Shady's mother's sobriety never lasted long once she had possession of her. Shady said the only reason her mother wanted her was to get assistance from the state, but she used all that money on drugs.

The last time her mother was able to get her was the last time she saw the preacher and his wife. Her mother relapsed, and they shortly found themselves living on the streets of Nevada, California, and Arizona. No one knew where they were living. She said they didn't know where they were living half the time. She grew up on the streets watching her mother chase drugs, prostitute, and steal what they needed. She said at one point, her mother had a pimp who protected them and let them stay in his house, but it didn't last long. All Shady knew was life on the streets.

One day Shady was digging through garbage searching for something to eat when the store's manager came out and ran her off. She said she hadn't eaten in over a week, and it was just trash to them. It should have been no big deal, and it made

163

her angry that the manager ran her off. So Shady took a knife from an outside restaurant table and went into the store to rob it. When the manager tried to grab the knife out of her hand, she stabbed his hand. She said it wasn't life-threatening or anything, just a surface wound. Not long after, she was arrested for armed robbery and later sentenced to ten years.

Shady stared at her shoes as she told me the story, and then she looked up with tears in her eyes.

"Rachel, from the day I was born, no one cared about me except for the preacher and his wife. My mom didn't want me, and I don't know who my father is. Why didn't the state just let me be with a family that could take care of me? Why did they keep giving my mother chances, knowing she didn't want me? My life would have been so different. I was never even given a chance at life. From the day I was born, I was trying to survive. The day I got arrested, that is all I was doing was surviving. Honestly, my life here is better than any life I lived out there. Someday it will be time for me to get out, but where do I go? Who am I getting out for? Before that day comes, I will commit a crime here. One that will get me more time because at least I have a place to lay my head and food in my belly while in here. Out there, I have nothing, I can survive this life, but I can no longer survive that one."

June.

June's story was the hardest one for me to hear because it resembled my own life so much. June told me that her father abused her mother all her life. She said her father was a police officer fighting crimes, but he was an alcoholic and abusive behind closed doors. She said her mother feared him so much because of his position, knowing that no one would believe the abuse. Her mother never worked outside their home; her father never wanted her to. They had nowhere to go, no money, and no way to get money. She said every beating her mother took got worse. She said her father would come home full of rage because of his job and then take it out on her mother, brother, and June. She said from the outside; their lives looked perfect. They lived in a lovely home, played sports; her father was a pillar of their community, but inside it was hell.

June told me that she spent most of her childhood dreaming about how to leave. She said she would wake up in the middle of the night sweating because she was running in her dreams. She didn't know where she was going; she was just running. She told me that her brother was quiet and took a lot of abuse from her father because he was a boy, but he just endured it and never said a word. They knew no other life.

One night her father came home at around eleven and started in on her mother. He pulled her out of bed and demanded she make him something to eat. After her mother fixed her father a meal, he picked his plate up, threw it across the room, and then forced her mother to crawl on her hands and knees and eat it like an animal. For the first time, her brother said something. A fight ensued between her father and her brother, her brother then picked up a beer bottle and repeatedly hit her father. Once they all realized what happened, they took her father's body, rolled it in a blanket, and carried it to the garage. They sat in the garage waiting for the right time. They gathered supplies and put her fathers' body in the back of the truck. They drove to a remote area and dug a grave. She said she thinks he was still alive when they buried him. They did their best to cover their tracks and clean up the mess, but their house was quickly taken over by the police when the news of her father's disappearance got out.

June's brother eventually confessed to what happened, implicating her and her mother. They were all arrested, her brother for the murder and her and her mother for accessory to murder. June was seventeen years old when the murder took place but was tried as an adult. When she arrived at Perryville, she was barely eighteen.

June told me that not one person asked why the murder happened. She said her father was given an honorable funeral with multiple police units and

166

people were standing on the streets watching. She said their entire town regarded him as a hero, but he was a monster, and no one wanted to hear it.

After each story, I would reflect on their circumstances. Where was the help they needed? After each tragic event, the system wanted nothing other than to lock them up. When these types of crimes take place, no one asks why they happened. Was it survival? Was it to protect an innocent child? What were the circumstances? See, the justice system only works for the benefit of those handing down the punishment. Many of the prosecutors, judges, lawyers, and even police officers have agendas. Many of them are friends and see their positions as just a job, which they want to advance in, sometimes at the cost of doing what is right. They believe they are serving their communities by locking people up for crimes, and in many cases, they are, but in many cases, they overlook the person behind the crime.

I realized that I am no different than any of these women. Although I am serving time for a crime I didn't commit; I could have easily committed it. During my abuse, I could have picked up an object to protect myself and killed Bryan. I could have been sitting here without a way out. Many times, I didn't see a way out of my marriage. I didn't have the resources or money to leave. I had two children and nowhere to go. I would have never been able to

167

beat a case like that. In thirteen years, I never once called the police on Bryan. I protected him and let him get by with it. Had I killed him, I would not have had a defense. I would have just been a murderer. Many of these women committed crimes because of circumstances, not because they were hardened criminals and ruthless individuals. Many of them were paying for what their parents did or didn't do. Many of them were children who were never given a chance to be children and grow into their full potential. It wasn't their fault, but they were paying the price.

Almost every one of these women was convinced to take a plea agreement. What that told me was they had no one fighting for them. I am sure an agreement was reached on a golf course somewhere or over a few drinks and then presented to them. With no money to fight, they had to take what was presented. There is no effort in a plea deal by the prosecutor or judge. A quick conversation, and then some legal secretary types it up. It makes me have no respect for them and what they are supposedly fighting for. That, to me, is not a fight.

For me, I was finding a new purpose. I would someday tell the world about all the wonderful women sitting in prison. The throwaways, the forgotten and useless. I would eventually talk about their kindness, their strength, and how they never had a chance. We don't get to see their goodness because the system locks them up and throws away

168

the key. Most of them are forgotten by their families, society, and even those they protected. Maybe someday we will see the person and not the crime, because everyone could be living a different life; circumstances are why we are not. We are all one decision away from a different outcome, a different ending.

Chapter 26
Release Day

As I listened to story after story about how the justice system failed so many women, one woman worked hard to get me released. I didn't know just how hard Yolanda worked on my case. She was let down many times and could have walked away, but she stayed at it, and because of it, she found Bryan's killer.

"Rachel, your lawyer is here to see you."
"My lawyer? Okay, I am coming."
"Hello, Rachel."
"It is good to see you, Yolanda. I almost thought you forgot about me." I smiled.
"I know I should practice better communication, but I wanted everything set in place before I came."
"Set in place?"
"Rachel, we found Bryan's killer. You are going home."
"No way. I am getting out for real?"
"For real. I need to give you something, though." Yolanda handed me two letters folded together. Disbelief came over me and then tears as I read the letters.

To Whom It May Concern,
My name is Jacob Miller, and as you may already know by your recent discovery, I murdered Bryan

Havens on June 3rd, 1988.

In January 1979, my baby brother Hank Miller was killed by Bryan Havens in Kansas. He was only twenty years old with a whole life ahead of him. His death destroyed my entire family. My mother and father were never the same, and my older brother and I were filled with anger and rage that we could not control. We were never given any answers to why he was killed, and I am not sure that it would have mattered.

I have spent the last eleven years preparing to avenge his death, a senseless death. I purchased a gun planning for the right time. For years I have followed Bryan and Rachel to every town and every state they lived in. I lost their trail at times, but I would soon pick it back up because they always somehow ended up in their hometown. Once I followed them to Pinetop, I realized that in order to get away with murder, I needed to insert myself into their lives. I did just that. I intentionally became friends with Bryan and soon after Rachel. I knew their every move, where they worked, where they shopped, and I even knew their chaos.

I did not know when, but I knew one day I would be given the opportunity to avenge my brother's death and I always needed to be ready. I was at the bar the night Rachel was drug out by the bouncers, and I knew that everyone thought she was crazy for what she did. I followed her home when her friend dropped her off. I sat in my car a few doors down, watching Bryan come home, and later the next morning, Rachel and her children loading a U-Haul truck. It was my opportunity, and I knew that all eyes would be on Rachel because of her actions the night before.

After Rachel and her children drove away in the truck, I drove to a secluded side road and parked my car. I walked back to the trailer and snuck in the back door. I found Bryan still sleeping in his bedroom, the trailer a mess and bare. I walked to the doorway of the bedroom and shot one time. He never even knew I was there. I quickly went out the back door and ran through the woods behind the trailer park. I was in my car driving away in a matter of minutes. I avenged my brother's death, and now Bryan's family would be destroyed and would always wonder why his life was taken.

I looked up at Yolanda, visibly angry. "Keep reading," Yolanda said softly.

My Dearest Rachel,
I am so sorry that you have endured such pain because of what I did. Unfortunately, that was my intention all along. I knew they would pin his murder on you. When I showed up at the courthouse for your sentencing, I was there to make sure I had got away with Bryan's murder, and later when I contacted you, I did so to keep making sure

I got away with it.

I didn't plan to develop a friendship and later falling in love with the woman whose husband I killed. In all my life I have never known anyone like you. The way you made me feel, the way you cared about others even though you had been done so wrong. I admired you, adored you, and yes, I loved you.

These last few years have been some of the best years of my life. I know that sounds crazy, but having you in my life, even if it was just letters and visits, was better than anything I have ever known. All I could think about was having a life with you, but the reality was for you to get out, I would have to go in.

I am not as strong as you, Rachel. I would never make it in a place like that, and truthfully, I never wanted you to know what I had done. It wasn't realistic to think that you would someday get out, and we would live happily ever after. I knew that all along, but I enjoyed thinking about it.

Maybe they would have caught me, and the result would be the same, but Rachel, I couldn't let you suffer any longer. You didn't deserve this, any of this, and I am so sorry. The last time I visited you, you said if only love could get me out. Love is getting you out, but I am not going in. Rachel, I hope someday you will find it in your heart to forgive me, but most importantly, I hope you find happiness in this life. You deserve every bit of it. With great love and regret, Jacob Miller.

I sobbed as I read every word Jacob wrote. I was used to his letters. He had sent me hundreds over the years. I was relieved, but I was heartbroken. Once again, I allowed a man to manipulate my mind and my heart. I don't know if I will ever be able to trust and love another man again.

"Rachel, gather your things. You are going home."

I was released from prison in April of 1996. I had spent over seven years locked up for a crime I didn't commit. As I reflected on all that had happened, I was angry, sad, and grateful.

Angry that there were so many people that could have helped me but chose to sit back or turn a blind eye to the injustice, and those that played a part in my conviction because of ego. Angry that I met so many people who were also wrongly convicted but didn't have the financial means to fight for their freedom. They could have been something great had someone fought for them and helped them. It continues to bother me to think of how many people sit in prison, trying to survive because they, too, had few options.

Sad because I found something that I was never able to find on the outside of those prison walls. I found people who genuinely loved me, who helped me without expecting anything in return. I formed friendships unlike any I had ever known. I was among great people who were never given a chance to show their greatness to the world. Sad because to have freedom, I had to leave those wonderful people behind.

Grateful for each of them and for the people who choose to fight for injustice in our system. People like Yolanda and Warden Johnson. People who believe in doing what is right when they could do wrong and further their careers. People like Jo, who encouraged me to take a leap of faith, who fought her own battles but stood beside me to fight mine. People like Pastor Mel who believed in redemption and that everyone is loved by God.

As I approached the gate, I felt the heat from the sun hit my face. I immediately saw my children and grandchildren on the other side. It was the most beautiful sight I have ever seen. So beautiful that I didn't see the fence or the barbed wire that wrapped around it. I could only focus on the thought of touching them and being with them again. I wanted to run to them as fast as I could, but I knew I couldn't. Until I reached the other side of that fence, I was still a prisoner of Perryville penitentiary. As the gate opened, we all embraced; tears flowed like water fountains as we rejoiced. Yolanda stood quietly, wiping her tears. I grabbed her and pulled her into our huddle. Yolanda was now a part of our family. I embraced her with a long embrace.

"You are one of the good ones; you did good. Thank you."

I sat in the back seat holding my grandsons' hand as we drove away from Perryville. I had longed to touch my grandchildren. They were more beautiful than the pictures. I was immediately in love.

"Mom, we don't fly home until tomorrow. Our hotel is close to the airport so it will take us a little while. The traffic is always bad around here."

"Can we make a pit stop?"

"Sure, wherever you want to go."

We pulled into the hospital parking lot. I had to see Jo before I left Arizona. She needed to see I was free.

"Ma'am, you can't come in here, only family."

"I am her sister."

"Oh, she has been expecting you."

"Damn, girl. You got out." Jo smiled her big sideways smile.

"I got out. They found Bryan's killer. It was Jacob."

"No shit. So, I guess he was a weirdo after all." We both laughed.

"I have missed you so much, Jo. Are you doing okay?"

"I might make it." Jo laughed.

"I am going back to Indiana. I won't be able to see you again, but I will write you."

"I would like that."

"You should see my grandchildren. They are more beautiful than the pictures."

"I am happy for you, Rachel. I am glad you are out."

"I have to go. Jo, thank you for everything you did for me. I will never forget you." I grabbed Jo's hand.

"Go do all the good you can do, Rachel."

"Bye, Jo." We both fought back the tears.

As for me, I returned to Indiana, where I was from originally. I enjoyed watching my grandchildren grow and catching up on all that I had missed over the years. With the help of my children, I opened a small bakery downtown. I named it Josy's Goods.

Six months after I was released, Jo died of a colon infection. She was thirty-two years old. The wounds from the attack she took from the gang members never quite healed, and infection took over her entire body. Jo's sister and I were the only two at her funeral; she had no one else. I laid a homemade apple pie on her casket as they slowly put her in the ground. Jo would forever be the person who helped me find my good.

Pastor Mel continued her ministry in the prison. The new Warden shut down her church, but she continued to minister to the women the best she could. She was doing all the good she could do.

Tori struggled to find her way after we were ripped from our pie-making. I later found out that she hung herself in her cell. She was never able to forgive herself for taking her son's life.

Sometime later, I began volunteering at women's shelters and traveling around, telling my story to women all over the country. I hoped to make a difference in this life. I wanted other women to know that they need to find the strength to get out of their situation, that they are worth it, and they are not alone.

I have learned a lot throughout my journey, and I will never take those lessons for granted.
I will never again hold respect for a person because of their degrees or position; you don't have to be a good person to have those titles. I will never take for granted the people who have shown me love, support, or given their time in my time of need. The people who have the least to give are usually the ones who give the most. I will never again have envy for those who are doing well. No one knows what battles they have fought to get where they are today. Sometimes we need someone to stand up and validate us to others. Forgiveness starts with forgiving ourselves. We all have something to contribute, find your good. Expect the good and bad days. They will come, but they will also pass.

Most importantly, I will always cherish my friendships and my family because we never know when we will see them again.

No matter where you find yourself in
this life,
do all the good you can do.

About the Author

Angela lives in Indiana with her husband, with who she co-owns a small trucking company. She also works at a local university where she is involved in mentoring young adults and actively participates in programs to bring sexual assault and domestic violence awareness on campus. She is a certified Green Dot instructor for the institution. The Green Dot training program teaches prevention on sexual assault, domestic violence and stalking prevention. Angela has been a writer most of her life, although she has only recently begun to publish her work. Angela is the proud parent of two grown children and grandmother to two adored granddaughters.

Photo courtesy of: Free your soul photography

www.ingramcontent.com/pod-product-compliance
Lightning Source LLC
Chambersburg PA
CBHW070852120626
46556CB00002B/964